THE DICKENS CONNECTION

CAMP HAWTHORNE BOOK THREE

Joyce McPherson

Also by Joyce McPherson

Books in the Camp Hawthorne series

The Pandora Device

The Revere Factor

THE DICKENS CONNECTION

CAMP HAWTHORNE BOOK THREE

Joyce McPherson

Cover design by C.T. McPherson

Published by Candleford Press

ISBN-13: 978-1534618572
ISBN-10: 1534618570

❧❨

To my children who have given me so much to
remember.

❧❨

≈≈

CHAPTER ONE

≈≈

My grandmother gave me the locket before I left. A round, gold disk no larger than a nickel with a delicate chain.

"What's this for?" I asked.

"For remembering," she said and gently opened the lid.

Inside was a tiny picture of my mom and dad.

"They were in Paris when this was taken," she said. "Your father gave the locket to her when you were born. The baby in the other frame is you."

I looked at my father's teasing smile and my mother's steady gaze that always reminded me of hope. "Thank you," I whispered.

Grandma wrapped her arms around me and hugged me tight. "I'll miss you, Stella."

"It's just a 4-H conference," I said, hugging her back. "I'll see you Tuesday."

A horn honked in the driveway, and she slipped the locket around my neck. "Go have fun," she said.

The van waited under our old oak tree, which was ablaze with orange and yellow. A few leaves floated down as I walked to join the others, and I took a deep breath of the autumn air, crisp with the first tinge of wood smoke. I waved one last time to Grandma and joined the others in the van.

"Did everyone bring enough warm clothes?" Lindsey's mother asked. She was usually easy-going, but she'd given everyone a strict packing list for the four-day trip with enough clothes to last us a week. She eyed Jayden's duffel bag, which looked suspiciously light.

"Jayden, you followed the list?"

"Everything but the coat."

"No worries—your grandmother gave me this." She handed him a coat wrapped in a clear plastic bag.

"How does she *do* it?" Jayden muttered as he stuffed it in his bag.

We pulled out of the driveway, and a surge of excitement zipped through me. After months of planning, we were finally on our way. The jars of strawberry jelly we'd made clinked softly against each other in their box, and the cinnamon of freshly baked apple pies blended perfectly with the smell of the pumpkin bread we'd made for the competition.

Lindsey twirled a bracelet she'd made from acorns and beads. "4-H, here we come!" she said, her blonde hair swishing as she bounced in the seat between Ellen and me.

Ellen was loaded down with notepads, pencils, a potato and a pair of dice on her lap. "Which game should we play first?" she asked. We had big plans for the hours in the car, and now that our families knew about our ESP powers, we could play modified versions of the games in front of them.

"Hot Potato?" Lindsey suggested. The game involved Jayden levitating a potato while we tried to catch it, but it was tricky in the car.

"How about Telephone?" I said. Lindsey linked us with her thought-transference skills, and it was hilarious when our messages got mixed up.

"No, I want to play a new game," Jayden said. "I call it Graveyard. It's like the alphabet game, but when we pass a graveyard, you don't lose points. Instead, Ellen has to tell everything she sees underground before we get out of range."

Ellen smiled, her braces sparkling. "I'm ready if you are."

I wasn't sure I wanted to hear about stuff buried at a cemetery, especially with my motion sickness, but we'd barely gotten to M and N before a police car pulled up behind us, siren wailing and light flashing.

"Everything okay, Mrs. T?" Jayden asked.

Lindsey's mom stopped the car and smiled back at us through the rearview mirror. "There's something I need to tell you," she began.

The policeman appeared at her window. He wore dark glasses, but he pulled them off to peer at us.

"It's Niner!" Ellen said.

Niner—our head counselor from Camp Hawthorne who turned out to be an operative with the Scientific Bureau of Investigation, the branch of the government

3

that investigated psychic phenomenon. I looked closer, and sure enough his silver badge read SBI. What was he doing here?

Lindsey's mom turned around, her eyebrows drawing together. "Sorry to break this to you, kids. But you can't go to the 4-H conference. Niner's here to take you to Camp Dickens."

"In England?" Lindsey squeaked.

"But the exchange program isn't till summer," I said.

Niner leaned through the window, his jaw clenched. "We can't always choose when emergencies arise."

I'd forgotten how irritating he could be. "Is this an emergency?" I asked.

"My orders are to get the necessary paperwork from your families and deliver you safely to our contact in London. That's all I'm authorized to discuss."

I looked at Jayden—brown arms crossed and shaking his head slowly.

"I knew something was up when they made us bring passports to the 4-H conference," Ellen whispered.

"Mummy, is this okay?" Lindsey asked in a small voice.

Her mother was rubbing the back of her neck, but she put on a bright smile. "It's okay, honey. Sorry I couldn't tell you sooner, but the SBI thought this might happen and wanted your families to be ready. Apparently, your team is needed."

Niner kept the lights flashing in the police car and raced all the way to the airport. I sat in the back seat with

Lindsey and Ellen, where the doors didn't have handles. Strange. I guessed it was for the criminals who had to ride there. Jayden sat in the front with Niner, but he looked back through the glass and rolled his eyes at us a few times. I knew he thought speeding was breaking the law, but it felt exhilarating to me.

In fact, ever since Niner appeared, my heart was thumping out of control. I felt for the gold locket and looked again at my parents smiling back at me. I was flying to faraway places, just like they did. Places with history and famous buildings and ancient stories...

Lindsey didn't share my excitement. She slumped next to me in the seat, like all her happiness bubbles had popped. "No pigs. No goats. No horses," she mumbled.

Ellen was biting her fingernails and turned to face her. "Sometimes you have to do things just because people need you," she said.

"But why us?" Lindsey asked. "There are lots of other kids from Camp Hawthorne with better skills."

"Niner doesn't want to tell us, but we'll find out on our own," I said. In fact, if my gift for seeing possibilities could help, we'd know as much as possible very soon. I just needed an angle. Possibilities didn't appear for regular events, like what you might have for dinner. The angle had to be something important, something that created alternate possibilities.

The first angle I tried was getting a read on our trip to the airport. I pictured us speeding along in the police car and then willed the next image to come. But I only got a nice view of the back of our heads—my bushy brown hair next to Jayden's crew cut—at the end of a long line at the ticket counter.

I visualized the airplane next, but that was fruitless. I'd never flown on one before. Instead I imagined us with our suitcases, and I got a brief flash of a red double-decker bus, but it fizzled out.

My head pounded with the effort, and I realized I was holding my breath. I let it out in a long sigh. I needed more information if I was going to find out what was happening.

఼ఴఴ

CHAPTER TWO

఼ఴఴ

We flew all night, and the sun was just rising over London when the plane circled before landing. Below us spires poked skywards and delicate bridges spanned the thick green ribbon of river like spider's webs. As far as I could see, buildings spread into the distance under the morning sky.

I wasn't even trying for a possibility when it came. I heard an ocean roar in my ears and my vision turned white at the edges as though the entire world was losing color. The images began flashing: the river on fire, black smoke pouring from buildings, then a gray haze covering everything. Nothing left.

"Stella!" Someone was shaking me. I wrenched myself away from the last bleak image and turned to see Jayden's face inches from my own.

He drew back his arm quickly, but his frown remained. "You were groaning," he said. "Is everything all right?"

The airplane cabin suddenly seemed too bright. I pressed my hands against my forehead, which was clammy with sweat. "I think I just saw a possibility for our mission, and it's not good."

Jayden listened as I described what I saw, his dark eyes squinting in the calculating expression I knew so well. "Niner wouldn't bring us here if we were really in danger."

But I wasn't sure about that. "What if he doesn't know any more than we do?"

Niner was too far from me while we waited in the cramped aisle to get off the plane, but I was determined to tell him about the possibilities at the first opportunity. He swept ahead of us through the long airport hallways but finally came to a stop at the line for customs. I caught up to him, and the others gathered around. "What would you think if I saw a vision of London on fire?" I asked him.

"Nice try, Stella, but I'm not allowed to discuss the mission."

"Why not?"

"First, you have to be briefed in a high security location, and second..." He stopped and scowled at a video camera on the wall. "They wouldn't tell me anything. Said it was for your safety. Excuse me." He hurried over to one of the security guards.

Ellen got the others to lean in. "London on fire doesn't sound too safe."

"Show me what you saw," Lindsey said. She got the images from my mind and passed them along.

Ellen was already pale from lack of sleep, but her eyes flew wide, and the last of the color drained from her face. "Do you think our families knew when they gave permission for us to come?" she asked.

"No way," I said. "But now we're here, we've got to survive."

I stared at Niner, still talking to the guard, and tried for more possibilities, but the only image I pulled up was him walking away.

It came true too, just a few minutes after we emerged from the train that took us from the airport. Niner strode up to a kid a few years older than we were.

"This is Alfie," he said crisply. "My orders are to bring you to him." He turned on his heel and walked back toward the train.

I ran after him. "Wait, Niner! Are you sure you're supposed to do this?"

He looked at his watch. "My mission is done. I have a plane to catch." Without a backward glance he stepped on the train.

I watched the doors close, a sinking feeling in my gut. What were we doing here? And how could I keep us safe?

The others were waiting with Alfie. He had sleek black hair cut like a bowl around his face. "Cheerio," he said, extending his arm to shake hands. "Welcome to jolly old England."

I shook his hand, and Ellen came next, tossing her red hair over her shoulder with a sniff. "Do you always talk that way?"

The corners of his mouth turned up impishly. "Would you prefer I talk like this—" He slowed his voice to an exaggerated southern drawl.

"Oh no," Lindsey interrupted. "I like the way you talk. I feel like I'm in a Jane Austen movie." She straightened her posture and glided forward to curtsey in front of Alfie.

He took her hand and bent over to press her fingers to his lips, and a choking sound came from Ellen's direction.

I glanced at Jayden from the corner of my eye. He was obviously enjoying the show. "I thought you'd be like James Bond or MI-5," he said.

"Shhh," Alfie said, lowering his voice. "MI-5 is a nasty word around here—like the FBI in America, only worse. We're connected with MI-7. The seven's for the seventh sense or extra-sensory perception."

"We call that the sixth sense in America," Ellen said.

Alfie raised a single eyebrow, a trick he must have worked hard to perfect. "In MI-7 we consider the sixth sense to be the mind. The seventh goes beyond that."

"So what now? Do we say *take us to your leader?*" I asked. Despite Niner's hurried exit, I was beginning to enjoy myself.

"No, you say *take us to your reader*. Follow me."

We left the train station, and the combination of cold autumn air and bustling city took away my breath. Buildings with shiny glass fronts rose around us, and cars, trucks and buses sped past in a dazzling stream of color.

Across the street a pedestrian stoplight signaled green, and I stepped down from the curb. A car engine revved, and I felt a yank from behind. "Not so fast," Alfie said.

A blur of black car, horn blaring, shot past the spot where I stood a moment before, and my heart pounded painfully in my chest. Did the car speed up and swerve toward me or was my head still muddled from the long airplane flight?

Alfie frowned, and I wondered if he had the same impression. "Remember to look both ways—cars drive on the left side here." He pulled me urgently by the arm to a bus stop where a red double-decker bus was just rolling to a stop.

"Ooh," breathed Lindsey. "Can we go up top?"

"Brilliant idea," Alfie replied. "Hop on, everyone."

The double-decker bus was just as I had seen in my vision. Inside, it had a narrow staircase directly behind the driver. I put away my worries about the crazy car and followed the others up the stairs, feeling as though some of Lindsey's happiness bubbles were percolating inside me. We squeezed into the two front seats, and the wide window brought us face to face with second-story signs above department stores.

"We could do some awesome shopping here," Ellen said.

I sat forward and tried to look everywhere at once. Signs for theaters, shops and pubs jumbled together with glassy high rise buildings. One of them had a sign that read "New Scotland Yard." The name reminded me of Sherlock Holmes and all the books I'd ever read about London. A tingle of excitement raced all the way to my fingers. I wanted to learn everything I could about this city.

The bus crept through the traffic, and beyond the modern buildings, two towers from a church appeared—as though they'd been plunked down straight from the Middle Ages.

"We're coming up on Westminster Abbey," Alfie said. "And there's Big Ben." The huge clock stood in the midst of spires and towers just beyond the abbey. The sudden change from modern offices to beautiful old buildings gave me the shivery sensation of entering a dream.

"What a place!" Jayden said.

Alfie pressed a button, and the bus slowed to a stop. "This is where we get off," he said.

We crossed the street and joined the crowd of people. They were everywhere—hurrying past on the sidewalk, standing in line to enter the abbey and milling around the square in front of the building. The towers I'd seen earlier framed the arched entrance. A huge stained glass window decorated the front, and smaller windows twinkled in the sunlight. The stone was carved in frills and fancy columns.

"Is this where we find the reader?" I asked.

"Righto. Westminster Abbey. Watch out for Saturday tourists."

We threaded our way through the crowd, and Alfie opened a smaller door in the side of the building. "For tour guides and MI-7," he said with a mischievous grin. "Check your luggage at the desk, please."

The inside of the abbey was even more impressive than the outside. Tall gray pillars rose above our heads, supporting graceful arches of gilded stone. Chairs were set up in front of a wall that looked like lace dipped in gold. I wanted to stop and study it a while, but Alfie hustled us off to a side room.

He stopped in front of a statue of a man leaning on a stack of books. "This is Poet's Corner," he said. "Many of our most famous authors are either buried or memorialized here."

The soaring architecture fascinated me, but Ellen kept jumping like she'd been stung and shuffling away from the group. "What's wrong?" I asked.

"There are *people* buried here," she hissed.

"Look at your feet," Jayden whispered. I stepped to the side and saw:

Charles Dickens
Born 7th February 1812
Died 9th June 1870

"You were standing on Charles Dickens," Ellen said, hugging her arms and standing with her feet together on a blank space.

Dozens of names were carved in the stone floor. Some of them were familiar to me, like Rudyard Kipling and Alfred Lord Tennyson. The leaning man was a memorial to Shakespeare. Carved busts decorated the walls and even the stained glass windows had names written on them. Lindsey was prowling around and pounced on an inscription set into the wall beside Shakespeare. "Look! Jane Austen."

"The tradition started when Geoffrey Chaucer was buried here," Alfie said. "In the UK we're proud of our authors. Though most people don't know about Camp Dickens, we do important work. And that's why you're here."

From the shadows behind a thick column, an elderly man appeared, walking hunched over a cane. He looked as old as the abbey, and I wondered if he lived there. "The coast is clear," he muttered.

"We'd best be on our way." Alfie still stood next to the plaque for Chaucer, and he reached over to press the letter C. The stone at his feet slid apart with a rasping sound to reveal a narrow set of stairs.

I hadn't eaten since dinner on the plane, and the rapid revelations made me slightly dizzy. Alfie's dark head seemed to bob down the stairs ahead of me like a bouncing ball. The steps were cut from uneven stone, and I kept a firm grip on the rope that ran along the wall for support. The trap door closed behind us with a hiss and a thud, and instantly a series of lights clicked on to illuminate the steps.

At the bottom of the stairs, lay the edge of a raised platform above a pair of long metal tracks. "This is a private branch of the London Underground," Alfie said. "Moulton has come from Camp Dickens to accompany us there."

Moulton seemed to wear a permanent frown. He harrumphed and tapped his cane on a wooden door set in the wall.. "Pick up your suitcases from the lift."

We pulled out our suitcases, and Moulton had us stand on a line painted on the floor. I had so many questions bubbling in my brain I didn't know what to ask first, but before I could begin, the train glided up to the platform, and Moulton hurried us aboard. "Everyone remain seated," he grunted. The door snapped shut, and the train blasted forward with a jolt.

The track had lights running along the side, but as the train streamed faster and faster, they blinked out, and I felt the familiar sensation of teleportation—roaring sound and blackness pressing in.

I peered ahead to catch the first hint of light, and it popped into view quicker than I expected—a half circle of green that grew and grew until I saw the stone frame of the tunnel and the dense bushes that lined the rails. We burst from the tunnel onto a track that stretched ahead, straight as a ruler.

But where it led I would never know, because a minute later the train pulled to a stop by a single bench on a short platform. The depot looked like an outhouse tucked behind a row of buildings, and it read *Chesterton Station* in faded letters.

"Our stop," said Moulton. He hobbled off the train and down an alley between the buildings to the main street of a village. It must have been noon by now, but the place was strangely quiet. A face appeared in one of the shop windows and quickly disappeared.

A boxy black car with a "taxi" sign on top was parked in front of the station.

"Put your suitcases in the boot," Alfie said.

Before I could ask what a "boot" was, Moulton opened the trunk for us.

"A boot must be the trunk," Ellen muttered.

Moulton got in the passenger side, which turned out to be the side with the steering wheel. It gave me an odd feeling to hear the car start and no one sitting in the driver's seat. We got in the back where two rows faced each other, and I took a seat next to the window, ready to see more.

Moulton drove so slowly I could have kept up on my bicycle, but I still didn't see much. I counted only four more buildings before the village ended at a gray stone church. It stood in the middle of a weedy plot of grass filled with crumbling gravestones.

Ellen shivered. "I don't think I'd want to explore that place."

"But you were going to play the Graveyard game in the states," I said.

"This feels different—layers and layers of peoples' lives piled on top of each other. Oh!" She jumped in her seat. "We just drove over a Roman shrine."

Alfie was watching her with an amused expression, one eyebrow quirked. "Most of the blokes with dowsing power turn it off until they want to use it. Too distracting to leave it on with all the early Romans, and Saxons and Angles and..."

"I get it!" Ellen folded her arms. "I never thought I'd be doing this, but here goes." She squeezed her eyes shut and held her breath for a moment.

"What did you do?" I asked.

"It's kind of like mentally turning off a radio. You cut the waves of data that pulse at you from the ground."

I wondered if it would work in reverse—if I could turn on a mental radio that would bring the possibilities faster. I closed my eyes and pictured the taxi, searching for a possibility, but nothing came.

After the church, we drove along a twisty road, bordered with tall hedges, mile after mile. Creeping along at Moulton's snail pace, we finally reached a wrought iron gate marked with a simple "CD." Moulton jerked the car to a stop.

"Camp Dickens," Alfie intoned. "Though everyone thinks it's for Charles Dickens. Brilliant cover." He slipped out to operate the key pad which opened the gate. Moulton eased the car inside, and the gate closed behind us with a clang. I stared at it and tried the mental radio again. A momentary image flashed in my mind of the gate at night and black dogs leaping around it. I tried to push the image farther, and I got a close-up of the dogs with their snarling jaws and wild eyes. I rubbed my sweaty palms on my jeans, and tried not to let the possibilities get to me.

Alfie was watching me intently. "Anything wrong?"

"Not at all," I said. There had to be an option for a good possibility soon, if I just kept trying.

❧❧

CHAPTER THREE

❧❧

Moulton drove slowly along a neatly cobbled path, also bordered with tall hedges.

"We'll be arriving soon," Alfie said. "Camp Dickens is like your own Camp Hawthorne and has replicas of the authors' homes for dorms. Charles Dickens recruited help from Robert Louis Stevenson, Alfred Lord Tennyson, Sir Arthur Conan Doyle and Jane Austen. You will be the guest of Dickens House."

Ellen's eyes lit up at the mention of Robert Louis Stevenson, but dimmed at the news we'd be at Dickens House. "Never heard of Dickens," she muttered. "And you can't see anything around here."

I was about to agree, but at that moment the tall hedge ended and we turned into a wide driveway. Moulton pulled to a slow stop in front of a tall brick mansion. The front door stood open and the bay windows on either side gleamed in the afternoon light. On top of the roof a cupola with a twirling wind vane sat like a tiny hat on a giant's head.

We climbed out of the car, and a plump woman with white hair darted through the front door, waving to us with a lacy handkerchief. "Welcome to Camp Dickens!" she called, her voice high and fluting.

"Everyone, this is Downey, our camp director and chef extraordinaire," Alfie said. He flourished his hand as though he was making a bow, and Downey smiled indulgently.

We introduced ourselves, and I tried to take a reading on the possibilities again. The leaping dogs at the gate burst into my mind, and I jumped slightly.

"Are you quite all right, dear?" Downey asked, gazing at me with a worried frown. "Perhaps a spot of tea? I'll have it ready in a twinkle." She disappeared into the house, and Alfie helped us get our suitcases.

Moulton, still wearing his scowl, pulled away in the taxi with a final harrumph.

"Cheerio!" Alfie called after him. "Rum fellow, isn't he?"

"Ah, the British," Lindsey said with a sigh. "Do you think we could learn to talk that way?"

Jayden shook his head at her. "Don't even try it— you'd sound funny."

"I don't *know*," I said, giving the last word a twist to sound as British as possible. "I might quite like it."

"Huh." Jayden had a way of communicating without words.

Downey had tea for us in a room she called the parlor. The wallpaper was pale green ivy climbing up a lattice, and the small tea table had a matching green tablecloth with a lace doily in the middle. I balanced my tea cup on my knee and tried not to spill it. The cup was painted with roses and had a delicate handle that looked like it might break when I touched it.

"You will be staying here at Gad's Hill Place, my dears, home of Charles Dickens."

I took a sip of tea, not ready for how hot it would be, and started to choke.

Downey patted me gently on the back. "We like to have our cousins from America visit us. Mr. Dickens and Mr. Hawthorne met through their dear friend, William Ticknor, who was publisher for both of them. For Mr. Twain, Mr. Whittier, and Mr. Longfellow, as well. Mr. Longfellow, himself, visited Gad's Hill Place."

I looked through the window at the wide green lawn and imagined Longfellow liking it here. It reminded me of his house back at Camp Hawthorne.

"And what do each of you do?" Downey asked, peering over her spectacles, which sparkled in the sunshine pouring through the window.

Lindsey had her tea cup halfway to her lips, but paused, obviously enjoying the pose. "Jayden is a telekinetic, Ellen is a dowser, I can read thoughts and Stella can teleport and…"

"Oops!" I bumped Lindsey's elbow and her tea slurped onto the green tablecloth. *Don't let them know about my possibilities.* I sent the thought to her mind while I fluttered my napkin and tried to mop up the spill. We were still strangers here, and I wasn't sure I trusted

Downey, even with her crinkly smiles and soothing way of talking.

Lindsey set down her tea cup and daintily wiped her lips with her napkin. "Everything is just so lovely here."

She smiled at me and I smiled back. *Good save.*

"If you like, Alfie will show you the grounds at Gad's Hill Place," Downey said. "You'll want to see the underground passage to Mr. Dickens's favorite writing spot."

Alfie appeared on cue, and I wondered if he was listening at the door—another good reason to be careful what we said. Until I knew what was going on, I wouldn't trust anyone.

He smiled and opened the door for the girls to go first, an irritating gleam in his eye that seemed to say *aren't I a swell chap to be so polite*? I ignored him and walked beside Jayden as we trooped out the door and across the lawn to a set of stairs leading down into the ground.

"Voila! The underground passage," Alfie said. "A friend of Dickens sent him a Swiss chalet for a gift—"

"A whole Swiss chalet?" I didn't think I heard that right.

"A small one. And he had it assembled on a piece of property on the other side of the road from his house. He had this tunnel built so he could slip away secretly."

The descent into the tunnel was like going down a rabbit hole. Though the walls were lined with stones, bits of moss and weeds stuck out between them, and we passed through semi-darkness underground. A hazy light glowed at the other end, where a matching set of steps took us back up to sunshine and grass.

The Swiss chalet looked like a child's play house—a tiny two-story building with white gingerbread trim under the roof. Steps on the outside led to the balcony on the second floor.

I opened the door and peeked inside. It was furnished with red couches and black bean bag chairs, and in the corner a half-finished game of chess sat on a table.

"We use it for a game room now," Alfie said.

"Doesn't it make you want to write here?" Lindsey asked. "I could curl up with my notebook for the rest of the week."

"Tea anyone?" Alfie opened a cupboard in the game room, and Jayden scowled.

"I can't get anything to eat here. Everyone keeps offering tea. Who drinks tea when they're thirteen?"

Alfie was poking through the cupboard, and I used the opportunity to pull Jayden back outside. "Something's going on. No one's telling us why we're here, and the longer we wait, the stranger it seems."

"Any possibilities?"

"That's the odd thing. Every time I try to see a possibility, I get an image of the gate at night and some crazy dogs leaping around it. Nothing else."

"We need to get to the bottom of this."

Jayden and I didn't have telepathy, but we understood each other. We marched back inside, and Jayden levitated the tea pot right out of Alfie's hands. I planted myself in front of him. "It's time to answer our questions," I said.

Lindsey and Ellen circled round—Lindsey smiling expectantly, Ellen with her arms crossed and a frown.

"Okay, okay. But let me make sure it's safe first."

We walked with him as he scanned the surrounding area and checked the room upstairs, then returned to the game room. Alfie closed the door.

"My instructions were to put it off as long as possible—"

"Who gave the instructions?"

"MI-7, of course." Alfie's tone grew serious. "It might be better if you didn't know."

"No way," Ellen said. "If we're going to help, we need the facts."

"It will make it harder."

"We like harder," I said.

Alfie sighed. "You were brought here because of the disappearance of Professor Jaeger."

I blinked. "Who?"

"There's a link between him and your team. Do you remember someone with the same last name?" The irritating twinkle in Alfie's eyes returned.

Jayden figured it out first. "Buckeye!"

Something in the back of my throat burned. I realized I must be more tired than I thought, but I couldn't let my emotions get to me now. Buckeye was our old camp counsellor, who travelled back in time to save his little brother from a rare cancer. After that, he'd joined forces with my parents working for the SBI until he was killed with them in the car accident. The familiar sadness washed over me, but I squashed it down and concentrated on Buckeye. Though my brain felt dazed, the links were clicking into place. "And the only other person we know with the same last name is… his little brother."

Alfie coughed. "Ah, he's not so little now. Actually quite grown up, and a distinguished new professor at Cambridge."

"So how do we get started?" Jayden asked.

Alfie added sugar to his cup of tea, a convenient way to avoid our eyes. "Actually, you don't. MI-7 asked the SBI to send you as bait. They figured the perpetrator would make a move on you because of the common history you share and give us a clue."

"So what do we do—just wait around?" Ellen asked.

"Yes, and pretend to be normal kids at camp."

"Ha!" I said. "What's normal?"

"There's one more thing. We believe there's an insider at camp feeding information to the enemy, so you can't let anyone know we had this conversation."

"We're supposed to be dumb, blind and useless," Ellen said with a snort.

✦✦

I was so tired by the time dinner came, I could barely lift my fork.

"You're suffering from jet lag," Alfie told us as he energetically buttered a roll and helped himself to another plate of food. "It's a combination of poor sleep last night on the plane and the time change—we're five hours ahead of the States, you know."

"How do you know so much about it?" I asked.

"MI-7 flies me all over the world," he said smugly.

"You can't be much older than us," Jayden said. "What do you do about school?"

"We have a private MI-7 school. They figure that kids are the best undercover agents."

"We're undercover agents, too," Lindsey said, her eyes brightening at the thought.

"Though *we* still have to catch up with school work when we get back," Ellen said.

I decided not to worry about it. The idea of being in England was glorious enough to blot out thoughts of missed homework.

The Dickens dorm had a curious ritual at the end of dinner. One of the older kids recited a short prayer and ended with: "As Tiny Tim observed…"

And everyone else chimed in "God bless us everyone!"

"Who's Tiny Tim?" Ellen said.

Jayden shook his head. "Haven't you ever seen *A Christmas Carol* on TV?"

Alfie seemed to swell in size. "One of Dickens's most popular characters is the poor sick boy, Tiny Tim. He was saved when old Scrooge reformed after being visited by three ghosts."

"It sounds more like a Halloween story than a Christmas story," she replied.

"Read it for yourself," Alfie said with a superior grin. He reached over to a row of books on the sideboard, all labeled "Dickens" on the spine, and pulled out the smallest one. "It's a short book."

"Maybe I will," Ellen said, tipping her nose in the air. She hated not knowing everything.

Downey made us go to bed right after dinner. "A good night's sleep will cure that jet lag," she said.

Our dorm was a large room with three canopy beds decked with lacy white tops. Each bed had a plump blue coverlet and little chest of drawers at the foot. I opened my suitcase to get my toothbrush and then stopped. Earlier, I'd put my parents' locket in the suitcase pocket, but it was no longer there. "Has anyone opened my suitcase?" I asked.

Lindsey was staring, forehead puckered, at her diary. "I'm sure I left my purple pen in here."

Frantically, I pulled out my clothes and realized they had been rearranged. My pile of shirts was mixed up with my jeans. "Someone's been going through our suitcases," I said, my stomach knotting at the thought of losing my locket. Why did I take it off in the first place?

Ellen, who liked to pack everything in a jumble, dumped out her entire suitcase. "I don't notice anything different." She started scooping it back in. "Though it does feel icky when someone goes through your stuff. Whoa—look what I found." She held up the locket on its gold chain.

"Maybe it's one of Scrooge's ghosts," she said.

I knew she was trying to get me to lighten up, but I didn't feel like joking. "More likely it's the bad guys we're supposed to draw out," I said grimly. I put the locket around my neck and felt its familiar weight over my heart. "I'm not taking this off until I know what's going on."

"I'll do some Dickens research for you," Ellen said, plopping on her bed with the book from Alfie.

"Aren't you exhausted?" I asked.

"Willpower," she replied. But even Ellen's determination couldn't overcome jet lag. I was still brushing my teeth when I found her fast asleep with the first page propped open on her pillow.

ৡৢৢ৶

CHAPTER FOUR

ৡৢৢ৶

Alfie rounded us up the next morning, and we walked into breakfast in the middle of a fight between two older kids.

"Get you gone, you dwarf! You minimus, of hindering knot-grass…" The girl paused, flustered, and the boy raised his finger at her, his face stern.

"More of your conversation would infect my brain."

Downey sat at a table calmly watching them. I couldn't believe she wasn't breaking up the fight.

"It's a Shakespeare insult contest," Alfie explained, leading us to a side table loaded with scrambled eggs and buttered toast. "The contestant who can spout the most lines wins. The girl will lose points because she forgot the last bit. It's *you bead, you acorn.* I was a camp champ once myself."

"Shakespeare wrote insults?" Ellen asked.

I giggled at the idea of the great Shakespeare putting aside a love sonnet to take up his feather pen and write a brilliant insult.

"Loads of them. They're in his plays."

"You mouldy rogue," the girl shouted.

"O braggart vile," the boy replied.

"Deboshed fish!"

We heaped our plates with scrambled eggs and toast and found places at the long wood table. The dining hall at Gad's Hill Place was more like a formal dining room than a camp mess hall. A fancy chandelier hung above us, and the walls were covered with pale green wallpaper, striped with narrow bands of white. "How do they fit all the campers in here?" I asked.

Alfie seemed confused by the question. "Do all the campers eat in the same place at Camp Hawthorne?" he asked.

"Yes, in a mess hall converted from a carriage house," Lindsey said.

Alfie waved a piece of buttered toast at the other people around the long table. "At Camp Dickens the dorms eat in their own dining rooms. Builds morale."

"What's with so many of the campers being old?" I asked.

"It's the beginning of a new term. College students get the first week off, and a lot of them come here to work for the Society for Psychical Research."

"Is that a real society?" I asked.

"Sure, the early members were British authors who helped start this camp—Tennyson, Doyle and Stevenson."

I was pleased that I recognized the names from Downey's chat yesterday, but another question was bothering me. "Are we the only kids here?" I asked.

"No, every house has at least four or five younger campers at this time of year, and we have contests as teams. You'll be glad to know that today we have a treasure hunt hosted by the Stevensons. They've already sent over the map." He unrolled it for us to see.

The treasure map was faded and smudged, but an X was clearly visible in the center. Someone had written in tiny letters "ten paces northwest and two paces south." The only recognizable symbols were a ship, a sun, and a palm tree. The map gave me a quivery feeling of adventure—perhaps England was a place where they found real buried treasure!

"I'll help with your team," Alfie said. "And I've brought T-shirts." He passed around red shirts with *Team Dickens* in huge white letters. In smaller letters, was the quote: "It is a far, far better thing that I do, than I have ever done."

"What's that mean?" I asked.

"Team motto," Alfie said with a satisfied smirk.

I tried to figure out why Alfie irritated me so much. Perhaps it was because he never bothered to explain things fully. Even though we spoke the same language, he made me feel like an alien from outer space.

Alfie took us to the treasure hunt by way of the cobbled road. "This road forms a circle," he said, as we left Gad's Hill Place behind. "Inside the circle is woodland, and outside are the dorms. Today we're going to the Stevenson place—Vailima. It's a replica of the house he built in Samoa."

We came around the curve to a breathtaking view of an island below us in the middle of a huge lake. The morning sun sparkled on the water as though the lake bubbled with magic.

"Island, ho!" Lindsey cried. We galloped down the slope and across the rope bridge that joined the pebbly beach to the island.

The dorm was a sprawling wooden structure that looked like two houses pushed together. Wide porches spanned the upper and lower levels, and grass hung in a fringe over them. A kid lounged against the railing of the upper porch and raised his arm in a sluggish welcome, then seemed to forget us and gazed back out at the water.

The other teams were already gathered. Alfie leaned in and spoke in a low voice, "Watch out for the Austens. They pretend to be mild-mannered, but they're devils in competition."

"Fancy a tea cake?" asked a girl, wearing the Team Austen T-shirt.

Alfie gave a slight shake of his head.

"No, thank you," I replied. We moved away from the other groups. "Shouldn't you tell us your gift?" I asked Alfie. "It might help with strategy, and besides, you know all of ours."

"Do I?" he said. "Your file was blacked out, you know. Or didn't you?"

I blushed and hid my embarrassment with another question. "Why keep it a secret? That Austen girl probably knows it already."

"I think not," he replied in clipped tones. "I've been recruited to MI-7, and my gift has to remain classified." He rustled the map, and we formed a tight circle around him. "Any ideas?"

"This is clearly a shoreline," I said, pointing to the squiggly line that separated a ship on one side from the palm tree on the other.

"And this is the sun," Jayden added. "Could be the east."

"Ah, a clever clue," Alfie said. "We turn like this so that east is aligned with the morning sun, and we ask ourselves, where can we find a shoreline that looks like this?"

Ellen had already figured it out and was running toward the beach where several wooden kayaks were stacked against a grass shack. "Can we use these? Please say yes!"

Alfie grinned and gathered up five oars. "You ever use a Samoan kayak? If not, get ready for a crazy ride."

The native craft had a long thin body that came to a point at each end. Alfie told us it was made from a single log, and I could believe it. Fortunately it had an extra piece of wood lashed to a plank on one side, about a paddle-length out, and it seemed to give the boat some stability.

"They're called outriggers," Jayden said. "I've read about these."

We had to take off our shoes and wade into the water to board them. Jayden held the boat steady with his telekinetic powers, but it taxed even his gift when the weight of the five of us tried to balance inside. I hardly dared to breathe. "Aren't we supposed to have life jackets?" I asked.

"The Samoans didn't invent them, but we do have floating coconuts if you need help," Alfie said.

I kept my paddle balanced across my knees and hoped we didn't tip.

"Now dip your oar like this," he said.

I'd learned to canoe at Camp Hawthorne, so the paddling was easy, but Alfie insisted we learn one of Dickens's water poems. "You're here as the guests of our house," he said. He recited one line at a time, shouting the dramatic parts with gusto, and we repeated after him:

> *The wind blew high, the waters raved,*
> *A ship drove on the land,*
> *A hundred human creatures saved*
> *Kneel'd down upon the sand.*
> *Threescore were drown'd, threescore were thrown*
> *Upon the black rocks wild,*
> *And thus among them, left alone,*
> *They found one helpless child.*

"What happened to the child?" Ellen asked, after we'd almost learned the whole verse by heart.

Alfie tapped his nose. "You'll have to read the rest for yourself. Now, one more time!"

We were still reciting as we drew close to the eastern shore. The first part of the land formed a rounded curve, but further along a huge rock jutted out. "It's like the squiggle on the map," Lindsey said.

We pulled the canoe onto the beach, and sat on the ground to put on our shoes.

Ellen had the map "Isn't it strange to have palm trees in England?" she asked.

Alfie shrugged. "They're not so unusual on the west coast of Great Britain where the Gulf Stream runs along the coast."

"The Gulf Stream?"

"A powerful current of warm water that starts at the tip of Florida and crosses to our coast. It makes for a milder climate here."

"So, I could send you a message if I dropped a bottle off the tip of Florida?" Lindsey asked.

"Theoretically."

Lindsey gazed off in the distance with a dreamy expression, then startled. "Look, a palm tree!"

It was tucked back from the shoreline in the middle of scattered pines. Though rather small for a palm tree, it sprouted a full head of curly fronds.

I reached up to touch them, and they tickled the tips of my fingers.

"This must be where we begin the ten paces northwest and two paces south," Ellen said.

Jayden oriented his body with the sun on his right and stiffly turned an eighth turn to the left. He counted ten steps, then turned abruptly due south and paced forward twice. "We dig here," he announced.

Only then did I realize we didn't bring a shovel.

"Why aren't other teams swarming around us?" I asked, thinking someone might share a shovel with us.

"Every team has a different destination," Alfie said.

Jayden had already found a stick to break up the dirt and was levitating the loose clods from the hole.

"Brilliant," Lindsey said, joining him with her own stick. I admired how she was already picking up the British lingo.

The rest of us joined them and began scraping at the spot. "We look like poor Ben Gunn," Ellen said with a laugh.

I leaned on my stick. "Who?"

"Haven't you read *Treasure Island*? It's the most exciting adventure ever, and it's by Robert Louis Stevenson. I was disappointed we weren't put in his dorm—no offense," she added to Alfie.

He grinned. "*Treasure Island* was my favorite too. Remember the sinister Black Spot that the pirates sent as a warning? And don't you love the part where Ben transfers the treasure to a different place and dupes the pirates?"

We'd cleared a hole about a foot deep, but no treasure in sight. "Wait," I said. "What if that's the point of this treasure hunt?"

Ellen unrolled the map again. "Where would the treasure go?"

"Ben hid it in a cave," Alfie offered.

"Look, there's a hump here we didn't notice before. What if it's a cave?"

Just then a spectral groan floated from deep in the woods. "Go back…" the voice moaned.

Goosebumps prickled on my arms.

"Go back…" I thought I heard the clanking of chains, and I looked at Alfie to see if this was normal. It certainly wasn't normal at Camp Hawthorne.

Ellen squinted into the woods, and a particularly agonizing groan expanded into a painful howl.

"That's it," Ellen said. "We're going in. No silly ghost voice is going to scare me." She stepped into the woods with us on her heels, when with a snap and a shriek, she was suddenly dangling upside down from a rope tied to the bough of a tree.

࿆࿆

CHAPTER FIVE

࿆࿆

Ellen's face turned as red as her hair, and it didn't help when Jayden tried to lift her right-side-up. "No, no, no! Cut me down."

Alfie came to the rescue with a pocket knife while Ellen fumed about good sportsmanship. "Haven't they heard about playing fair in the UK? What would Downey say?"

By the time she was standing back on the ground, Alfie was laughing. "You can't expect to win a treasure hunt around here as easy as that. There's got to be challenge, you know."

"Of course," Ellen said. "But wait till I have the chance—I'll get back at whoever did this."

Alfie was studying the knot in the rope. "If I had to guess, I'd suspect the Austens. I told you how competitive they are, and Jane Austen's brother was an admiral— knew all the fancy sailor knots like this one."

I scanned the woods for the camper behind the spectral voice, but couldn't spot anyone. "We've got to find that cave if we want to win," I said.

Ellen gritted her teeth. "Ha! This was just a fun game before, but now it's personal—we're going to find that treasure!"

She pushed through the low-lying branches of pine and shrub, and the others followed, but Jayden hung back. "Do you think it's suspicious—someone luring us farther and farther from our boat? I don't like it."

"What should we do?"

"I'm going back to guard the beach and mess around with the hole some more. Send for me if you find the treasure and need help." Without waiting for my answer, he slipped back the way we came.

I ran to catch up with the others. Alfie insisted on going first and checking for more traps, but he didn't find any. The cave was just a hump of earth with a hole as high as my knee. "How do you hide treasure in there?" Ellen asked.

Alfie crouched down and peered inside. "There seems to be something with a rope handle." He reached in to pull it, and several things happened at once.

"Do you hear that?" Lindsey asked. "Sounds like humming…"

At the same moment Alfie gave an enormous tug and pulled out a large rock, wrapped in rope. A black circle was painted on its surface. Ellen shrieked, "The black spot!"

The only thing I knew about the black spot was it was BAD. Before I could even step backwards, an angry buzzing erupted from the hole, and a swarm of yellow bees attacked.

"Run!" Alfie shouted.

Bees were crawling on my neck, my face, my arms, stinging through my thin jacket. I tried to swat them away, but it just made them mad and the attack intensified.

"The lake!" Alfie yelled, crashing somewhere off to my left. I spurted ahead and stumbled onto the beach.

Jayden was nowhere to be seen, but I didn't have time to look for him. With yells and screams, we jumped in the icy water and sank below the surface. Even then, a few determined bees stung. Finally, it stopped.

I stood up, panting for air, feeling as weak as a baby. Water dripped from my hair, and I was shivering from the shock of the freezing water. My jeans protected my legs, but my face and neck were throbbing. I tore off the jacket and saw large red welts rising on my arms.

"Wasps," Alfie said, between breaths. "They don't die when they sting. Nasty customers."

Ellen's green eyes took on her ferocious tiger-look. "Our game was tampered with," she said. "And I'm out for revenge."

I tried to picture the mild-mannered Austen girl who offered us tea cakes cooking up this diabolical plan, but I couldn't do it. I searched the possibilities for where we were heading, but once again I got the image of the gate at night with snarling black dogs. I shuddered. Perhaps this was more sinister than a simple kid's game.

"Where's Jayden?" I asked, glancing at the hole. It was larger, and something had been dragged out of it and across the dirt. Jayden wouldn't need to drag anything, but he might… "Quick, everyone. We need to follow this trail. Someone's trying to steal our treasure, and Jayden is following them."

The drag marks led back into the woods. I took the lead this time, too impatient to let Alfie do his safety stuff. He whispered a warning about traps, but I shushed him.

The farther we ventured, the thicker the trees grew until the sunlight was almost completely blotted out. The ground was harder here, and I had to walk bent over to make sure I didn't miss the track. I was so engrossed in following the trail, I almost blundered into a huge log that barred our way. Gouges in the bark showed where a heavy object slid across it. I climbed up, ready to continue the search. On the other side lay a crumpled shape.

"Jayden!" I turned him over gently, and he groaned. A huge bruise was forming over his left eye. "Are you all right?"

He staggered to his feet. "Where are they?"

"Who?"

"The little people." Frantically, he crawled on hands and knees and scraped away the pine needles. "They sank through the ground here. It must be here."

Ellen helped him, checking the ground with her dowsing powers for a ten-foot radius.

"Tell me what they looked like," she said.

Jayden rubbed his head and closed his eyes. "There were three of them—the size of kindergarteners, but they looked like adults. And they wore green."

"Are you sure you didn't get a concussion?" I asked. "Maybe your memory isn't quite right."

Jayden glowered. "I know what I saw. I got back just as they were dragging our chest into the woods. I followed, and a tall guy with a hooded cloak joined them here. When I thought they weren't looking, I tried levitating the chest back to myself, but he had stronger powers. He lifted me over the log and sent the chest flying at my head. The last thing I saw was the little people laughing and sinking through the ground."

Ellen finished her search and shook her head. "I can't find anything."

I put my hand on Jayden's arm and summoned the possibilities once more. Surely, they couldn't fail me at a time like this, but I couldn't pull up anything.

"Something's blocking our powers here," I said. "Ellen, try again."

This time Ellen picked up two sticks and crossed them in front of her. Immediately, they began to wobble, but they didn't pull her toward the ground. Instead, the sticks dragged her deeper into the woods, so fast that we had to run to keep up with her.

I was right behind her as we broke from the woods into a clear blue sky—only five feet from the edge of a sharp cliff.

"Drop the sticks!" I yelled, grabbing Ellen's sweatshirt and digging in with my feet to hold her back.

She thrust them away from her, and the sticks fell over the cliff to a rocky creek far below. The height sent my head spinning, and I dragged Ellen backwards.

"I don't like this," I said. "We've got to get back to the boat."

But when we returned to the shore, our kayak was almost completely submerged, and the side float was gone. Jayden flipped it over for us, and Alfie inspected the damage. "Someone cut the outrigger from the canoe. We're going to have quite a balancing act to get back across the water in this."

I pulled Alfie aside. "Do you think this is related to our mission as bait?" I asked.

He clenched his jaw. "I'm not sure, but we need to be more careful in future."

By the time we reached the Stevenson house at Vailima the other teams had found their treasure and were celebrating with a picnic. There was a lot of good-natured teasing when we returned empty-handed, but apparently the Stevensons were more into having fun than completing the mission. The teams displayed their open treasure chests next to the food table.

"Coconuts?" Jayden said "The treasure was coconuts?"

One of the Stevensons picked up a hairy coconut and cradled it in his arms. "They're great for crafts. You can carve a creepy face on them and hide them in the girls' dorm for a lark."

I didn't feel like hanging around the picnic, so I excused myself, saying I needed to get into some warm clothes. The girls went with me, but the boys stayed for the food.

Downey took one look at us, with our dripping clothes and red blotches from the wasp stings, and insisted on hot showers. We put on fresh, warm clothes, and she fussed over us, dabbing the stings with a sweet-smelling ointment and pouring us cups of strong tea with lots of sugar. When at last we protested we were fine, she suggested an afternoon of quiet reading.

She took us to the library, which was a fascinating place. Books covered the walls from ceiling to floor, and in front of a bay window stood a wide desk.

"Is this where Dickens wrote?" I asked.

"Everything just as he left it, dearie, and look at this." She closed the door to reveal the back side, disguised as a bookcase, giving the illusion that the room had no entrance. "A little conceit of Dickens," she said, her face dimpling into a smile.

Lindsey was turning in slow circles. "I don't know where to start."

"The camp authors are featured in this bookcase. It's been kept up even after Mr. Dickens' death."

I strolled along the wall, dazzled by the hundreds of books. I paused at the secret door to read the titles and realized they weren't real books. One series was called *The Wisdom of Our Ancestors* and had numbered volumes: *I Ignorance, II Superstition, III The Block, IV The Stake, V The Rack, VI Dirt,* and *VII Disease.*

Ellen joined me. "Look, how thin he's made *The Virtues of Our Ancestors.* Dickens must've been my kind of adult."

The books on the far wall were unusually tall and thick, but when I turned in that direction Downey paced in front of it, her hands fluttering nervously. Instead I settled on the bookcase with the camp authors. Lindsey was there and had picked out her favorite Jane Austen book—*Pride and Prejudice.* I found *Treasure Island.* Ellen muttered something about the poem Alfie taught us and loaded herself down with a stack of poetry books.

"Ready, doveys?" Downey asked in her comfortable voice. She turned the knob on the secret door, and it swung open. Walking through the doorway, I glanced back into the book-lined room. A shadow seemed to flit across the far corner, but Downey swung the door closed before I could be sure.

She brought us more tea, and we curled up on chairs around the fireplace in her parlor. The smoke was sharp and bitter, like nothing I'd smelled before.

Lindsey took a deep breath and sighed contentedly. "A wild and mysterious smell."

"What kind of logs are these?" I asked.

"Not wood at all," Downey said. "It's peat. We cut it from the turf in the bog."

"Bog?" I was fascinated with all the new words.

"A sort of swamp—not a place you want to visit yourself," she replied.

She bustled off, and the three of us settled into the soft cushions on the couch by the warmth of the peat fire. Lindsey paused before opening her Jane Austen novel. "I think Alfie likes you," she said dreamily.

"Yes," Ellen said. "Haven't you noticed how he always walks by your side?"

"Bosh," I said—a useful word I'd already picked up from the Stevensons. I bent my head over *Treasure Island* and was soon lost in the exciting adventure of Jim Hawkins. I'd reached the place where a mysterious blind man visits the inn with his sea chest, when Ellen gasped. At first I thought another wasp had followed us inside.

She closed her book with a snap. "Can you believe this Dickens guy? You'll never guess what happened to the helpless child in the poem Alfie taught us!"

Lindsey was reading with a fluffy pillow on her lap, and she leaned forward and intoned the first line in a deep voice: "The wind blew high, the waters raved. A ship drove on the land…"

"What's the rest of the story?" I asked before she could finish the entire poem.

Ellen brandished the green volume at us. "It's totally unfair. A kind old sailor cared for him, but the sailor died, and then another took over, but the boy died next. Weren't happy endings *invented* in Dickens' day?"

"Of course they were," began Lindsey, but Ellen interrupted her.

"There's another thing—are we expected to do nothing after all the dangerous stuff this morning? You can't tell me those wasps were part of the game. Or the attack on Jayden."

"Or the crazy sticks," Lindsey added.

At her words the image of the vicious dogs at the gate floated into my mind. "I know we're only supposed to be bait," I began slowly. "But I don't intend to sit around and wait for the next attack."

"Me either!" Ellen said, chucking the poetry book on the table. "You gotta make your own happy endings."

"I have an idea from something I saw in the library," I said. "But we need to sneak in when Downey isn't watching."

Lindsey volunteered to check on Downey in the kitchen with the excuse of getting another pot of tea. "Though if I drink any more tea today, I'm going to float away," she said.

She returned with the tea pot and a tray of cookies. "Downey is busy making these—she calls them biscuits," Lindsey said.

I bit into one, and it was sweet and buttery, better than the sugar cookies I had at home. The others munched on biscuits while I explained the plan. "Our goal is a section of tall books on the back wall. I thought I saw one with MI-7 in the title."

"Isn't MI-7 supposed to be secret?" Ellen said.

"Yes, but remember they send a lot of college kids to research for that psychical society here. Perhaps they let them study those kinds of books. I tried to get closer to the shelf, but Downey kept pacing in front of it."

"Let's go," Ellen said. "If we get caught, we'll just say we're looking for more to read. I'm done with poetry, for sure."

Outside, the sky had turned a dusky gray, and the hallway was dark. We made it to the library without meeting anyone, but I stopped short at the sight of an older kid sitting at the desk. Under the glow of a green desk lamp, he was reading and taking notes, papers scattered around him. They rustled as though a gentle breeze was passing over them, but the window was closed. He finished a note and floated the page to a pile on the side.

"A telekinetic like Jayden," I whispered to the others.

Lindsey sent a thought to us. *I'll ask him questions and you go for the book.*

Ellen and I nonchalantly sauntered toward the far corner while Lindsey stood at the boy's elbow. "Excuse me. I wondered if you could tell me where to find books by Jane Austen," she said.

The boy turned his head to speak with her, and I slipped the book from the shelf and onto a nearby table in one smooth motion. The title read *The History of MI-7*, and my heart thumped with excitement as I opened the cover and scanned the table of contents.

Ellen, her eyes wide, pointed to a chapter titled *The Suppression of Psychic Phenomena in Great Britain.*

I flipped through the pages, passing tantalizing headings like *Clairvoyance in Espionage* and *Telekinetics in Battle* until I reached the chapter. I read silently, "The suppression of psychic phenomena in Great Britain began in the mid-nineteenth century with the pioneering work of Charles Dickens, who considered the paranormal powers to be too dangerous for the general public. He proposed the formation of a secret organization, which later became MI-7. He also founded a camp to train students who manifested an aptitude for basic skills such as mind-reading and levitation. Under Queen Victoria the administration was well-regulated, but at the turn of the century new problems arose and the danger of…"

Watch out, Stella! Lindsey's warning came just in time. The boy stood up and was looking in our direction. Ellen and I hurried forward, leaving the book in hopes he wouldn't notice it. Lindsey was smiling and bobbing her head. "I want you to meet Oliver. He's here from Oxford on a study break."

Oliver had sandy hair and a jaunty smile. "My work is on Dickens and his experiments with mesmerism."

"Mesmerism?" Ellen said.

"Americans call it hypnosis. It was named for Franz Mesmer who believed there was an energy, or life force, that transferred between all living things."

"It must be fascinating to study," I said.

Oliver took a step toward his notes, his eyes suddenly wary. "Not really something young campers should be hearing about. Why are you here anyway?"

"Just getting more books," Lindsey said. "Downey's letting us read by the fire."

At the mention of Downey, he seemed to relax. "Nice to meet you," he murmured and returned to his paper-strewn desk.

I strolled back to our book, hardly daring to breathe, hoping he wouldn't stop us from our research. Ellen reached the book first, and her face grew pale. "Someone has changed the page," she whispered.

The book now lay open to a chapter near the end, and resting on it was a glossy brown nut, like a monster acorn but without the cap. I picked it up and rolled it between my fingers. "Why is this here?" I asked.

Ellen squinted at it. "Maybe a clue." Her eyes grew wide, and she pointed to the top of the page where the nut had rested.

Dr. Bruce Jaeger and the Life Force

The newest research on the life force involves the possibility of healing tissue at the cellular level. The work is pioneered by Dr. Bruce Jaeger and builds on early research by Mesmer and other scientists. His laboratory operates under the authority of MI-7, and the project is not made known to the general public.

"Do you think Oliver did this?" Lindsey asked.

I glanced at his desk, but he was gone.

"Why wouldn't he do it openly?" Ellen countered.

"And regardless of who turned the page, why did they want us to know about Bruce Jaeger?"

We were still staring at the page when Alfie and Jayden strode into the library.

"What are you doing?" Alfie asked.

I wrenched my eyes from the book. "Just enjoying the library."

"We were looking for you everywhere." He tossed a ball toward me, and I managed to catch it. "I brought you the winning ball from our cricket match."

"How gallant," Ellen said, grinning at me like a Cheshire Cat with braces. I pretended not to notice.

Alfie took one look at the book we were studying and snapped it shut. "Didn't Downey tell you this section is off-limits to campers?"

"No, she didn't," I said, lifting my chin in the air. "Why should it be?"

"What have you read?"

"Only a couple pages of history."

"Good. Some of this stuff is classified. You could get in big trouble with MI-7."

"Why didn't Downey warn us?"

"Probably too busy."

Something about Alfie's manner annoyed me. Did he think he could waltz in and charm me with some grimy ball and then boss us around? I slipped the smooth brown nut into my pocket without showing it to him.

Jayden must have sensed the tension, and he put on his heartiest voice. "You missed a great picnic. We played a new game called cricket."

The distraction worked. Alfie punched Jayden in the arm. "Not a new game, old chap. We've been playing it over here longer than you've had baseball. We won handily thanks to you."

"Any clues about who booby-trapped our treasure hunt?" I asked.

He shook his head. "It's a rum thing—no one admitted to making the ghostly voice or setting the trap. Usually everyone wants to brag about their tricks."

"I think it's the mole," Ellen said. "Tomorrow we'll be on our guard, and they won't be able to trick us so easily."

༄༅

The rest of the day passed without further mishap. For dinner Downey made us shepherd's pie with real lamb in it. I'd never tasted lamb before, but it wasn't too different from other meat. It was mixed with carrots and peas and topped with mashed potatoes that were crispy and brown. I thought of my parents trying new foods like this when they traveled to far off places, and I touched the locket, seeing their smiling picture again in my mind. It was exhilarating to follow in their footsteps.

After dinner we had a ghost story in the parlor. Alfie turned off the lights so the only illumination came from the burning embers in the fireplace.

"Not too far from here," he began in a solemn voice, "there were reports of a huge black hound with phosphorescent eyes that hunted down and killed every member of the Baskerville family. Sir Arthur Conan Doyle thoroughly researched the tale and discovered that it began three hundred years ago when Hugo Baskerville, famous for his despicable deeds, was killed by a demon hound."

He paused and looked around the room, the fire casting a reddish glare on his face.

"The curse fell on the entire family," he continued. "One descendant after another died under mysterious circumstances—the last one from a heart attack with a horrible expression of fear printed on his face. Sir Arthur Conan Doyle was asked to help when the new heir moved into the family home."

He made his voice hollow as he told the gruesome details, and my scalp prickled creepily when he described the midnight chase on the moor and the hound baying mercilessly. I was so engrossed in his story that I jumped when some of the ashes settled in the grate. It sounded like demons hissing from hell.

After the story, Alfie said the only proper way to end the evening was by candlelight. We made our way up to our rooms with just the flickering flame. I caught my breath every time we turned a corner and our shadows leapt tall.

"I'm not sure I'm a fan of ghost stories," Lindsey quavered, as we tiptoed around our room with the candle, checking for intruders or anyone going through our suitcases again.

Downey bustled in, took one look at our scared faces, and flipped on the lights. "Nonsense," she said when Ellen explained about the candlelight. "What you need are some nice hot bedwarmers."

It turned out that bedwarmers were a lovely British invention—like a small pillow filled with rice. Downey brought them already heated and flurried out again with some more bedwarmers for the boys.

I was just putting mine under the blanket at the foot of my bed when a chorus of barking sent me running to the window.

Lindsey pulled her covers over her head with a squeak. "It's not the hound of the Baskervilles, is it?"

Outside I caught a glimpse of a distant light. "It looks like someone with a flashlight walking along the road."

"It's probably Moulton doing his rounds," Ellen said sleepily. "Downey told me he walks the perimeter of camp every night with his dogs to make sure it's safe."

I shivered. I didn't really believe in the hound of the Baskervilles, but were those the same snarling dogs from my vision?

≈୬ఞ

CHAPTER SIX

≈୬ఞ

At breakfast a gilt-edged envelope arrived. "To the campers of Gads Hill Place," it read in swirly handwriting. Downey passed it to me, and I caught a whiff of perfume—lavender perhaps?

"Oh my goodness!" Lindsey gushed. "Is that what I think it is?"

"I have no idea what you think it is," I said, but she snatched it away before I could even discover what she meant.

She pulled out a stiff cream-colored card and waved it in my face. "It's an invitation to a vintage ball hosted by the Austens! With lessons this morning to prepare us." She jumped up and did a gliding sort of dance on the spot, but stopped suddenly, her face stricken. "What will I wear? I thought we were going to a 4-H conference and didn't pack anything suitable..."

Downey stopped by on her way to the kitchen. "Not to worry, dearie. Mr. Dickens had daughters you know. We'll find you a lovely dress."

Ellen huffed at all the fuss. "We need to use this dance to focus on finding the mole," she said in an undertone.

"And a camper from the Austens is probably our best candidate."

Jayden scowled. "It's not a mole we need to find—it's the little people."

"There's no such thing as little people," Alfie said with a superior smile.

Jayden clenched a fist on the table, and I moved closer in case I needed to stop a fight.

"It could be both," Lindsey blurted.

Everyone looked at her, and she blushed. "You said there was a tall person there, too. Maybe the mole is one of the college kids, and he's in league with the little people."

"Just be on guard when we visit the Austens," Ellen said. "This may be our chance to find the mole."

Alfie shook his head. "It's best not to meddle. Your mission is simply to serve as bait."

I didn't agree, and from the way Ellen's jaw jutted forward, I knew she agreed with me. We would do our own research, and Alfie didn't need to know.

We started off for the Austen dorm, going the opposite way from yesterday on the cobbled path. Lindsey had wanted to dress up for the morning dance class, but Downey said the dresses must be saved for the ball.

Lindsey didn't seem to mind. "The perfect day," she said with a sigh. "I love everything about Jane Austen— the manners, the dresses, the romance." She stopped in the path so suddenly I stepped on the back of her tennis shoe. "Was Jane Austen psychic?"

Alfie drew himself up, putting on his professorial act, and Ellen rolled her eyes. "Actually, we don't know. It was her brother, Henry, who asked to help with Camp Dickens. Jane died before he started this place, but she asked that any profits from a certain novel she was writing be used for young people with sensitivities similar to her heroine, Catherine. The novel was published after her death with the title *Northanger Abbey*. Have you heard of it?"

"A wonderful story," Lindsey exclaimed. "Catherine imagines all kinds of spooky things when she visits an old house and gets into trouble because of it. She marries her true love in the end." Lindsey did a few more swooping dance steps. "I can't believe I'm really here."

"Believe it. There's the Austen dorm," Alfie said.

A mossy wall, about as high as my shoulders, held a neatly trimmed lawn dotted with clusters of flowers and bushes shaped like balls. Set cozily in its midst was a red brick house with greenery growing up the walls.

"Welcome to Chawton Cottage," he said.

It was funny how houses had names here. The cottage had a white door, and all the windows were open. Someone laughed inside, and the door flew open like the flap on a cuckoo clock.

Out stepped Oliver, only today he was wearing a top hat and a plum velvet coat with tails. I stopped short, unsure what to say. Should I ask him about the book in the library and the page someone turned? But if he didn't do it, then I might expose the person who was trying to help us.

Lindsey came to the rescue by making a grand curtsey. "Are you here for the dance class?" she asked.

I'd always wondered what the word "rakish" meant, but now I suddenly knew, because Oliver tapped the top of his hat and grinned rakishly. "I'm the dance instructor himself," he said. "Won't you join us in the drawing room?"

The drawing room was the main room of the cottage. Couches and chairs had been pushed against the wall to make a clear space in the center. The Austen girl who offered us tea cakes yesterday sat at a small piano. "Amelia is our piano accompanist," Oliver said.

She waved and launched into a lively tune.

"Line up," he called, "gents on one side, ladies on the other."

"Aren't the other campers coming?" I asked.

"The Austens already know the dances," he said. "And the Doyles can't come because the game's afoot and the Stevensons are helping them."

"What about the Tennysons?"

He shrugged. "Probably late. You know the poetic types."

Once we were in two lines facing each other, Oliver taught us a series of dance steps like *do-si-do* and *swing your partner*, and then walked us through a pattern that ended with the lead couple making an arch for everyone to go under. He called the steps over and over until we had run through it at least five times. By the end, I knew all the steps and could relax and watch how fancy it looked when we danced in unison.

"There's only six of us now," Oliver said. "But wait until tonight when thirty people are dancing at once."

He gave us a break before he taught the next dance, and I asked Amelia, who still sat at the piano, where I could find a bathroom. She giggled. "Do you want a bath?"

I must have looked confused because she didn't wait for an answer. "The toilet is down that hallway, next to the girls' dorm room." I made a mental note to ask for the "toilet" next time.

Somehow all the little differences like "boot" and "toilet" made me feel grumpy. Why couldn't we all speak English the same way? I stalked down the hall but stopped short at the door to the girls' dorm where a hunched figure was rummaging through a desk. Was that Moulton? I peered around the doorway—it was definitely Moulton, and I was certain he was not supposed to be there.

I watched as he shut the first drawer and moved on to a second desk. He seemed to be looking for something because he studied each piece of paper, even holding some up to the light. I wondered if he was looking for hidden writing. The floor squeaked, and I turned to see Amelia walking toward me, her face tilted with concern. "Everything all right? I'm sorry for teasing you about the bathroom."

Drat! Moulton would know we were there. "I'm fine," I said, trying to keep my voice cheery. "I was just curious about how your dorm was set up. I see you have a desk for each girl."

The girl smiled shyly. "Yes, Miss Austen believed that everyone needed a little space for writing."

"I like that idea." I casually peeked back in the room, but Moulton was gone—an amazing trick for a man his age.

Amelia and I returned in time to start the next dance with the Tennysons who had arrived at last. It was a repeating pattern with everyone changing partners as they danced in a circle. Jayden was my first partner, and I told him about Moulton. He frowned. "We need to keep an eye on him. I'll tell the others."

He danced with Ellen and Lindsey in turn, and I glimpsed him speaking with them as I sashayed with my partner and twirled on to the next one.

Lindsey sent a message to my mind: *Jayden says to keep this among ourselves. Don't tell Alfie.* It was an odd request, but I'd been through enough adventures with Jayden to trust him.

The Austens had lunch for us—little sandwiches with interesting fillings. One was cucumber and cream cheese, and another was water cress. There was hot tea of course, which made Jayden shake his head and wince.

On the way back to Gad's Hill Place, we cut through the woods that grew in the center of camp. The thick gray trunks stood like columns supporting a canopy of orange leaves above us, and the ground was covered with hard round nuts, identical to the one I found on the MI-7 book.

Lindsey scooped up a handful and jiggled them in her cupped hands. "What are these?"

"Haven't you seen a horse chestnut tree before?" Alfie asked.

"We call them buckeye trees in our country," Ellen said, not to be outdone.

Alfie picked up one of the glossy brown nuts. "*We* call these conkers, and they're prime fun. You've never played with them?" He squinted at us as though we were teasing him.

"Never," I said.

Alfie harrumphed in a perfect imitation of Moulton. "I guess it's my duty to teach you, then. Try to find the hardest conkers you can, and bring along five or six."

I filled a pocket with the smooth nuts. They had a hard casing but a soft underside that was lighter brown.

Alfie took a screwdriver from his pocket. "I always carry one of these in conker season," he said. "Shoelaces, too."

He showed us how to whittle through the nut, starting from the soft side until we pierced through the middle. Then he produced brown shoe strings for each of us to thread through the hole and knot at the end.

"The first person is called the striker," he said. "He gets to hit his opponent's conker until he misses. Then the other person has a turn. We'll have a practice round first."

He had me dangle my conker at arm's length. Then he wound his string around his fist a couple times and held the conker tight at the end of the shortened string.

"Tchah!" He whipped it down and the two made contact, bouncing madly through the air. We inspected both conkers, but neither had broken.

"I get another go since I hit your conker," he explained.

He missed, and I got the next turn. I wound the string as he had and tried to lash it at his conker, but I missed by a mile.

The next round his conker cracked against mine and burst open. "You win," he said with a rueful grin. "Now you have a one-er because it's won once. The rest of you have none-ers until you win. Then you can become a two-er and so on."

We had a contest under the rustling chestnut trees, and the winners of each round played against each other. Lindsey squealed when the conkers smacked, but she won every time.

Ellen was disgusted. "You'd think there'd be more skill involved, but it's just the luck of having the tougher nut."

Jayden quickly mastered the game, developing several elaborate new ways to swing the conker.

"You must represent our team in the tournament," Alfie said. "Even if we don't win, we'll have the most brilliant moves."

After my first victory, I lost every round and had to sit out the finals. I sat with my back against the rough bark of a tree, breathing in the smell of damp leaves and peat smoke. Squirrels chittered in the branches above me, and I watched the gold and orange leaves swishing in the wind.

Jayden joined me on the ground. "Alfie's a great guy," he said.

"Then why aren't we telling him about Moulton?" I whispered.

"Just being careful. Alfie lectured me last night how we can't solve this ourselves. He says we must leave it to the authorities, but I think he's afraid we'll find something we shouldn't." Jayden swung his conker so that the string wrapped around his arm. "He still doesn't believe there were little people." He rose to his feet in the fluid motion he did so well and rejoined the others.

I watched the end of the tournament with only half-interest. I still had the conker from the library in my pocket. I rolled it between my fingers, thinking about all that had happened since we came to England. We were like conkers in a way, dangling from strings as bait for whatever evil was out there. I hoped our team was tough enough to win without cracking, but the waiting sent an undercurrent of tension spinning through every day.

Even under the peace and beauty of the spreading branches of the chestnut trees, I couldn't shake the feeling that we were being watched, and the watcher was out to get us.

We walked back to Gad's Hill Place as the sun sank over the woods. "It gets dark earlier here," I said.

"Winter's coming when the days go dark before dinner," Alfie said gloomily. He was still swinging his conker on the string. "Odd coincidence about conkers. You call them buckeyes in the states, and Buckeye was the nickname of Bruce Jaeger's brother, wasn't it?"

I nodded and felt for the round nut in my pocket. Could there be a connection?

≈⋙

CHAPTER SEVEN

≈⋙

Downey rushed us through dinner and then took an extraordinarily long time getting us ready for the vintage ball. It wasn't enough to button us into gowns with tight bodices and long skirts, but she had to curl our hair and arrange bits of it on top of our heads. "I want you to look just like Mr. Dickens's daughters," she cooed, stepping back to gaze on her handiwork.

I felt like a clown, with curls clustered on either side of my cheeks, but Downey clapped her hands. "You look just right! And your locket completes the look."

I felt for the locket which dangled down the front of my dress. What would my parents think if they could see me now? I was really and truly in an adventure, just like they used to have.

Downey wore a kindly expressions, her head tilted to the side. "What do you keep in your locket, my dear? A boyfriend perhaps?"

"No, a picture of my parents." I opened the locket for her and she stared at the miniature photo, surprise flickering in her eyes for a moment, but she quickly concealed it. "Such a lovely couple. I'm sure they miss you while you're here."

"They died a long time ago."

"Oh, I'm so sorry." She seemed flustered by my revelation and looked around the room distractedly. "I almost forgot the gloves," she gasped. "I'll return in a twinkle."

I was still wondering at her strange behavior when the others arrived. Jayden wore a gray tailcoat and a frown. "I can't swallow," he said. "Alfie tied the necktie too tight."

Alfie wore a matching jacket and carried an ivory tipped cane. "Buck up old chap. All in the line of duty." He smiled at me, and I pretended to be busy with my locket.

Lindsey floated into the room in a pale pink dress with ribbons tacked along the bottom. Her face was flushed to match her dress, and her words came fast and shrill, like a firecracker about to explode. "Isn't this amazing? Downey said there will be dance cards and punch and flowers for the girls."

Downey brought us long gloves, and Ellen helped me pull mine on. "Remember to keep your eyes peeled for clues," she whispered. "We'll do our own sleuthing, though Lindsey will probably be useless."

"She can't be that bad," I muttered, but my gift of possibilities clearly wasn't working because I completely misjudged the enchanting effect of a vintage ball on my friend.

"I think I'm going to swoon," Lindsey announced as we entered the drawing room at Chawton Cottage. It was filled with girls in swirling skirts and boys standing stiffly with neckties too tight. Amelia played a lilting waltz on the piano and swayed slightly to the music. Oliver was calling a dance, and Lindsey waved at him. "Isn't he marvelous?"

"Who?" I asked.

"Oliver," she said, with a breathless sigh.

Ellen rolled her eyes. "He's too old for you."

"Not in Jane Austen's time," Lindsey said. "The gentlemen were older and established."

"May I have the honor of this dance, Stella?" Alfie asked, one eyebrow quirked and his trademark grin. "I may not be much older, but I'm an established dancer."

"Dance with Lindsey first," I said, feeling the blood rush to my cheeks. "I'm still trying to figure it out."

Alfie nodded reluctantly, and the two of them joined the line of dancers.

That left Jayden, Ellen and me. We looked at each other and burst out laughing. "I'm not dancing if I can help it," Jayden said.

"I think I need to check something on my dress," I said loudly. Then in a lower voice: "This is our chance to investigate the Austens. Jayden, you look for clues in the boys' dorm, and Ellen and I will check the girls' dorm."

The hint of a smile flitted across Jayden's face. Despite his telekinetic powers, he was a miserable dancer.

Ellen and I edged around the room, pretending to watch the sashaying partners. When we reached the hallway that led to the girls' dorm, I pointed to the fastening on my back and Ellen nodded energetically. If anyone was watching us, they ought to be convinced.

We made it to the girls' dorm without meeting anyone and slipped inside.

"This is where I found Moulton," I whispered to Ellen. "Let's look at the papers and see if we can figure out what he was doing."

We each took a desk, and I gasped when I opened the drawer. On top of a stapled bunch of pages lay a glossy conker. "What do you make of this?" I asked.

Ellen inspected it. "No hole. Perhaps it's being saved for a game?"

I glanced at the packet underneath, which was an article torn from a magazine. "Mesmerism and the Universal Life Force," I read. "Isn't this what Oliver was researching?"

"And look at the author—Professor Bruce Jaeger."

"What would it be doing in a girl's desk?" I asked.

Someone knocked at the door, and we froze. "Put everything away," Ellen whispered, eyes round with panic.

I slid the drawer shut just as Alfie opened the door and poked his head around it. "Lindsey was looking for you," he said.

Ellen patted my back as though she was arranging something. "We were just fixing the fastener on Stella's dress."

"Shall we return to the dance?" he asked, extending his arm to me.

I smoothed down the front of my skirt and placed my hand on his arm as Oliver had taught us to do in dance class. I was grateful for the gloves Downey had given us. My pulse was racing and my palms were sweating. For some reason, I felt nervous around him.

Jayden was already back in the parlor, sipping a glass of punch in a huddle with a group of boys.

"It's the lads from the cricket game," Alfie said. "If you'd excuse me, ladies."

"That was odd," Ellen said. "Why'd he bother to get us if he was just going to talk with the boys?"

"Jayden said he doesn't want us trying to solve the mole problem on our own," I said.

Lindsey floated over, still waltzing as she came so that she looked like a ship bobbing at sea. "Did you get your flower? The Austens are handing them out, and Oliver gave me mine." She brushed the bloom against her cheek.

"Were you looking for us?" I asked.

"Why would I do that?"

Ellen gritted her teeth. "We went looking for clues, but Alfie brought us back here with some nonsense that you wanted us."

I turned my back on Alfie and the group of boys and talked fast. "Lindsey, we need you to go back to the girls' dorm and search the desks. We'll explain later."

She glanced at Oliver, who was rounding everyone up for another dance. "Do I have to go now?"

"Yes. You can dance all you want when you get back."

"All right, dear Stella," she said in a voice like one of our Jane Austen movies. "Take care of this for me." She gave me her flower to hold and glided out of the drawing room. I wondered how she moved so smoothly in a dress. Maybe she had other powers still undiscovered. Floating? Gliding?

At that moment the flower tugged out of my hold and floated up to tap me on the head.

"Where'd you get the flower?" Jayden teased.

"Careful with that—it's Lindsey's, and she got it from Oliver."

"Oh." He let it drop back into my outstretched hand. "I thought Alfie gave it to you."

"Why would he do that?"

"He likes you—he's always asking where you are."

"Ha!" Ellen said. "Lindsey was right."

"That's not why he's asking," I said. "He's trying to keep us from finding out things for ourselves."

Jayden tugged at his tie and grimaced. "Did you find anything in the girls' dorm?"

"An article by Professor Jaeger, and the strange thing was—it had a conker on it."

"What was it about?"

"The same stuff Oliver is researching—mesmerism."

"That's interesting. I didn't find anything in the boys' dorm, not even the papers from Oliver's research."

Ellen raised an eyebrow in perfect imitation of Alfie. "Why would he keep it somewhere else?"

"Perhaps he's connected to our mystery," I said.

Lindsey slipped into our circle, two red spots forming on her cheeks. "I searched the room, but Amelia walked in before I could find anything. She said Alfie was looking for me."

Jayden squinted at Alfie and the guys, still in a huddle by the punch. "I don't know what Alfie's up to, but we're not the kind of bait that waits around doing nothing."

I agreed with Jayden, but for the rest of the evening there didn't seem to be anything else to do but dance. Amelia gave me a dance card, and lots of boys from the other dorms signed up. I liked the Doyles best. They were young and a good six inches shorter than me. They talked the entire time—saying they knew I came from the States because of my accent, and I was from Dickens's dorm due to the cut of my dress, and on and on. I pretended to be impressed with their sleuthing powers, and they all called me Irene for some reason. I made a note to read more of the Sherlock Holmes stories when I got the chance. I hadn't encountered Irene in the mysteries I'd read so far.

Near the end of the evening a Tennyson boy asked me to waltz. He was murmuring lines of poetry when Jayden strode up and tapped him on the shoulder. "May I cut in, old chap?"

The boy startled and bowed to me. "Better to have loved and lost, and all that," he muttered.

I took Jayden's arm to continue the waltz. "I've never seen someone cut in before," I said.

He wore a pleased smile. "A little trick I learned from Alfie."

"He's up to something."

"Yeah—he won't let you out of his sight. No more sleuthing for you, but I have an idea. Oliver's papers have to be on the premises. I'm going to check the little room with the bookcases."

"Great plan," I said. He twirled me under his arm for the fancy finish of the dance, and we didn't do too badly. I could almost understand Lindsey's enchantment with the dance.

Jayden picked his way through the crowd on his way to the door, and I took out my dance card to check who had signed up for the last dance. It was Alfie. The feeling of enchantment melted away.

I tugged my gloves back into place and searched the dancers but couldn't find him. Jayden made it to the doorway and slipped out of the room, and I caught a glimpse of a matching gray tailcoat following him down the hall. Alfie must have been guarding the door. I needed to warn Jayden.

Everyone lined up for a reel, and I tried to push through the people on the fringes, but they were packed too densely. Fortunately, there was another way. The dancers had formed two long lines facing each other and were bowing in place. Before Oliver could call *swing your partner*, I dashed through the middle and out the door, a gentle murmur swelling behind me. I'd probably broken all the rules of good manners. A boy shouted after me: "Did you see Irene?"

The hallway was empty, and I tiptoed along it toward the little book room, thankful for the ballet shoes Downey insisted we wear. Jayden and Alfie were talking inside.

"Why don't you believe I saw the little people?" Jayden said, his voice urgent and low.

"It doesn't matter. I just don't want anyone to get hurt. Stella's idea to find the mole herself is bosh. Let the authorities do their work, and do your part to draw out the baddies."

"What aren't you telling us?"

"Nothing, but these are dangerous blokes. They…"

Alfie's voice dropped, and I stepped closer to hear.

Jayden was facing toward the window, and his body tensed. "Wait, there's someone hiding out there," he said.

Alfie looked where he pointed and shrugged. "I don't see anyone." But his voice wasn't convincing.

"He's huge." Jayden opened the window and leaned out.

"What are you doing?" Alfie said. "I told you there's danger!"

"The bait plan is working," Jayden said, his voice grim. "Call your contact at MI-7."

"Wait!" But Alfie was too late. Jayden had already climbed out the window.

I ran into the room and peered out. The giant figure of a man was barely visible, loping away from the house with Jayden in pursuit. Jayden was fast, but he was faster. He must have been over seven feet tall, and despite his uneven gate, he could have been an Olympic runner.

I hitched up my skirts and swung a leg over the windowsill.

Alfie grabbed my arm. "I'm not letting you go. This is England, for heaven's sakes. We don't let women run into danger."

He sounded like Downey at that moment, and I regretted having to ignore him, but Jayden needed my help.

I shook off his hand and hopped from the window ledge, then hiked up my skirts and sprinted after Jayden.

Beyond the patch of light from the windows, the Austen garden was almost pitch black. The dim half-moon kept me from blundering over the round bushes, but I realized I'd need a better way to track the runners. I found the mossy wall that surrounded the garden and dashed out the gate. Running my hands along the top of the wall, I jogged beside it. I hated to think what my gloves would look like when we got back.

The wall ended and I paused. I didn't know where to go next. In the dark I might walk in the wrong direction, and then I'd be no help at all. I listened for even the slightest movement, but the only sound was the wind rustling the bushes.

I imagined Jayden running and tried to find a possibility of where he could be, but the snarling dogs at the gate leapt into my mind again. I quickly squashed down the feeling of panic ballooning in my chest.

Reaching into the space in front of me, I found something that felt like a hedge. I walked slowly along it, crouched low and keeping my other hand checking for obstacles in the path. It was slow progress because the ground dropped away steeply, and I kept stepping on my long skirt.

Suddenly, an unearthly howl sounded ahead of me. I muffled a scream, my hand on my mouth. "Jayden?" I quavered.

I heard a moan and walked downhill toward it. "Jayden?" In the dark I stumbled against something.

"Stella?" He spoke as soft as a sigh, and I was never so relieved to hear his voice. "Do you have something I could use to stop the bleeding?"

"Is it bad? What happened?" I had to talk to keep myself from getting hysterical. I whipped off my glove. "Try this." My hand brushed his leg and came away sticky with blood.

"Thanks for coming after me," he said. I heard the snap of the glove being tied in a knot, and he groaned. "Your tourniquet works great. Could you help me walk back?"

I took a deep breath to steady myself. "Hold on." I helped him stand, and he put one arm around my shoulder so that I could support his weight. We'd been friends since we were little, but I wondered when he'd become so heavy. He grunted with every step on the bad leg. "Can you use levitation to help?" I asked.

The pressure on my shoulder seemed to lessen, and we walked slowly up the slope toward the lights of the Austen house. Jayden was breathing heavily, and he signaled to stop for a moment. We were close enough to the house that I could see the pain on his face now. He bent to tighten the tourniquet and looked back down the hill. "He got away when I gashed my leg on a branch," he said.

"Could you see him at all?"

"No—only that he was tall enough to play professional basketball."

"Do you think he's the one we're trying to draw out?"

"If he is, this is serious…"

"Who's there?" a gruff voice hailed us. A flashlight played on the path, and I saw Moulton with three dogs. They were black like the snarling dogs at the gate, and I froze. They ran forward and snuffled around us.

"Jayden's hurt," I said. The dogs brushed against me, and a rising fear threatened to erupt in a scream if they pounced, but they quickly lost interest and returned to their master.

"What were you doing down there?" Moulton said, his voice stern.

"There was—" I began, but Jayden interrupted.

"I thought it would be fun to explore the garden at night. Didn't realize how steep it was."

Moulton harrumphed. "That's dangerous ground. You shouldn't explore when you don't know the place."

"Can you help him?" I asked, impatient with the lecture when Jayden clearly needed help.

"Aye, come in the kitchen."

He didn't scold us after that, though he did squint at Jayden's muddy dress pants and tailcoat and harrumphed a few more times. He cut the ruined pants from around the wound, so that one pant leg ended above the knee. "Good work stopping the bleeding. No bones broken, but you could've bled to death," he said with grim satisfaction.

He unwound the bloody glove, and I almost experienced one of Lindsey's swoons. I sat on a kitchen chair and waited for the room to stop spinning. One of the dogs came and sat by me. He was much larger and older than the other two, with a grizzled snout and warm brown eyes. I patted his bristly fur and he sighed contentedly and lay down on my feet.

After that I felt better and could watch Moulton's operation. He cleaned the cut with alcohol and wrapped it with white bandages that he produced from one of his many pockets.

"He likes you," he said, nodding toward the dog.

"What's his name?"

"Henry."

He whistled softly and the two dogs snoozing near the fireplace leaped up, but Henry kept sleeping.

Moulton rubbed his back. "Come along old man," he said. Henry opened his eyes and tried to stand, but his back legs were weak. Moulton bent stiffly and supported him to his feet. "Quite a pair, aren't we?" His voice sounded sad, but he straightened up again and frowned at me. "I'll drive you home."

"I should tell Alfie we're going," I said.

"No need—he asked me to look for you while he took the others back. Babbling about a giant, he was." He peered at me under his bushy brows, and I was startled by the clearness of his gaze. Did he know more than he was telling?

≈≈

CHAPTER EIGHT

≈≈

Downey insisted Jayden stay in bed until noon. He wasn't happy about it. "Downey's always bossing us around," he grumbled when I brought him his breakfast tray.

"You'll get better faster," I countered. "And you can use the time to figure out what's going on."

He picked at his scrambled eggs with a fork but didn't eat any. "Alfie said he called MI-7 but their operative couldn't find anything."

"Don't you think the entire episode was strange?" I asked. "Moulton knew about the giant but didn't ask more questions. What if he's in on it?"

"I'll think about the possibilities while I lie here—if it won't be intruding on your territory."

"Don't worry—the only possibilities I'm getting lately are those horrible dogs."

≈≈

Since we didn't have any scheduled events for the morning, Downey offered to teach us to make scones in the kitchen. Ellen excused herself, saying she'd gotten to the exciting part of *A Christmas Carol,* but Lindsey and I accepted her offer.

The kitchen was a cozy mixture of old-fashioned wooden counters and gleaming modern appliances. Geraniums bloomed on the window sill, and a cherry-red dish cloth hung drying by the sink.

Downey brought out canisters of flour, sugar and raisins, which she called *currants.* She kept up an easy flow of conversation, explaining why she used only *real butter,* and showing us how to measure the flour on a neat little digital scale. "Much more precise than measuring with a cup," she assured us.

The trick to good scones seemed to be *cutting in* the butter, which was trickier than I imagined. Downey gave us each a pastry cutter, which looked like the letter U made from six narrow strips of metal attached to a wooden handle. We were supposed to cut the butter and flour mixture with the tool, over and over, until it looked like pea-sized balls of butter coated with flour. Lindsey quickly got the hang of it, but my bowl looked more like a heap of sawdust.

Downey's face puckered in doubt at the sight of it, but then she giggled. "We'll just see how it comes out!"

We mixed in the rest of the ingredients, kneaded the dough a few times, and then rolled it out on a pastry cloth that covered the wooden cook table. We cut circles with upside-down glasses, which I thought was clever.

As we put the scones in the oven, a copper kettle began to whistle. "A spot of tea is just the thing mid-morning," Downey said.

We sat at the cook table and sipped our tea. The warmth from the stove and the buttery smell of baking scones created an island of peace after our first busy days.

"I was meaning to tell you something," Downey said, pouring some cream into her cup. "I recognized your parents in the locket yesterday."

Though I had put two spoonfuls of sugar in my tea, it suddenly tasted bitter in my mouth. My tea cup clattered back into the saucer. "You knew my parents?"

"Not to say I knew them," she said. "But they were exchange students here when I was camp counselor—oh, twenty years ago or so. It was the year before I became eligible for the MI-7 exam, and I had such hopes." She paused and shook her head. "I thought at the time they might be sweet on each other, but they weren't much older than you are now."

She sipped her tea and studied my face as though looking for something. "If you're like your father, I guess I know what your other gift is."

"I didn't say…"

"I know—we like to keep things to ourselves, but you can't keep secrets from old Downey."

"I think I better check on Jayden," I said, rising so quickly my chair fell backward. I shoved it back under the table and scuttled out of the room.

Why was Downey so determined to know our gifts? And why did she think I had a second one? I needed to talk to Jayden about the conversation. He was an excellent strategist and would know how to handle it. But when I peeked around his door, he was asleep. I'd have to discuss it with him later.

I walked back to my dorm room to ask Ellen's advice, and Alfie popped out of the library. "I've got a special activity for you," he said. "Meet me in the long hallway upstairs in fifteen minutes."

I arrived to find Alfie wearing white from head to toe—a white long-sleeve jacket, white pants that ended at the knee, and white knee socks. "I'm glad you wore jeans," he said, throwing me a matching white jacket. "Today is fencing class."

I put on the jacket, and he picked up a thin sword like the three musketeers used, whipping it through the air to make an invisible X. "This is called a foil."

"Whoa, you could hurt someone," I said.

"No worries. You'll be wearing a mask and there's a rubber tip on the end—see?"

I examined the foil and saw a tiny black rubber tip. It wasn't reassuring.

"Besides, it bends like this." He demonstrated by poking my chest in the region of my heart. I yelped and jumped back, but not before I saw that it was true. The foil bent and didn't even pierce my jacket. Alfie laughed.

He explained that you got points if you made a "touch" against your opponent. But only certain zones counted. "Whipping the legs is not allowed," he said sternly.

"But they don't care where they slash each other in movies."

Alfie squared his shoulders, and his face stiffened. "Fencing is not a brawl. It's an art, like mental chess. Downey asked me to teach you because she thinks it will help with your extra sensory powers. A kind of cross-training, if you like."

Downey again. Was she trying to get me killed? I sighed and put on my mask.

Alfie started by teaching me how to lunge and keep my sword arm straight. The free arm had to hover behind my back with the hand curled on level with my head. It actually looked rather dashing.

Then he hung a tennis ball from a rope in a doorway and had me lunge and try to touch the ball with the tip of my foil. It was a lot harder than it looked. Though the air was chilly, I was sweating by the time he said we could try a match.

"We begin by bowing like this," he said.

I bent stiffly and tried to copy his moves, holding my foil ready.

It was strange staring at Alfie in a mask. You couldn't tell what he was thinking. The mask was round like an astronaut helmet, but with mesh in the front. It reminded me of the blank face of a robot.

Alfie darted forward and his foil came straight for my heart. In a flash I saw a picture in my brain of my own foil swiping his away. I swept my arm with the foil held straight, and Alfie sprang back and whipped off his helmet.

"That's brilliant! Have you fenced before?"

"No, just getting the hang of it."

"Well then, let's begin."

He bowed again, and this time I was ready for his first jab. He got in a few touches, but I made a few myself.

"You never told me your gift," he said as our foils clacked against each other.

I faltered, and he got in a jab, but it glanced off my arm.

"You never told me yours," I replied.

He lunged, and once again I saw in my mind's eye a way to avoid it. I turned my shoulders sideways to dodge his foil.

He growled in frustration. "You're too good if it's true you've never fenced," he said. "I think I can guess your gift."

My arm froze in mid-air. I was seeing possibilities again in place of the barking dogs! What had changed?

He plunged his foil at my shoulder. "Touch!" he yelled, and I bowed and backed away.

Playing with Alfie was more dangerous than I anticipated.

I was so intent on the game, I didn't notice Ellen had joined us, but Alfie stopped abruptly and pulled off his helmet.

"Yes?" he said coldly.

Ellen frowned. "I'm sorry to interrupt, but Downey sent me to get you for lunch."

Alfie forced a chuckle that sounded more like a cough. "Silly me, I let the time slip away."

I looked at my watch, and it was noon already. We had fenced for two hours.

I peeled off the white jacket, soaked with sweat, and looked at Alfie to ask what to do with it, but he was far down the passageway, striding toward the dining hall.

"He's rather intense, isn't he?" Ellen said.

I giggled. "Do you think he's going to wear his fencing gear to lunch? What will Downey say?"

At lunch Downey pronounced Jayden well enough to go around on crutches. "The wound is healing nicely, and the swelling is almost gone," she said.

Jayden celebrated by dashing across the room on his crutches.

"Just so long as you don't overdo it," she added.

"Not to worry—we're going to visit the Doyles today," Alfie said.

He took us along the cobbled road in the direction we had gone yesterday to the Austen dorm. A short distance beyond the cottage lay a stylish row of town houses. The shiny black door in the middle read 221B.

Jayden gasped. "That's not 221B Baker Street, is it?"

"Elementary, my dear Jayden," Alfie replied.

The crutches clattered to the ground, and Jayden placed a reverent hand on the door. "I never thought I'd see this place in real life."

"It was a little joke from Sir Arthur Conan Doyle," Alfie said. "He didn't think any of his homes ranked with the other authors' houses, so he insisted that old 221B represent his house here. We fitted out the entire place with dorm rooms, but we kept Sherlock's rooms the same."

Jayden would have bounded up the stairs if his crutches allowed it. As it was, he used the handrail and one crutch to hop from stair to stair until he reached the first landing. It was an impressive feat, and I figured he was using his levitation to help.

On the first door, a small brass name plate read *Holmes*.

"May I?" Jayden asked, his eyes shining. He limped into the room and turned slowly to look at every detail. Then, as though a spring had let loose inside him, he hobbled from one item to the next. "Look, his pipe and the Persian slipper where he kept his tobacco. His violin." A strangled yelp. "Here's the dummy head he used to lure Moran—you can see the bullet hole."

The dark wood furniture and red wallpaper glowed in the gas light. The oriental carpet on the floor, Holmes' famous deerstalker hat on the table, the fire flickering in the grate—all cast a quiet feeling of comfort.

"Cheerio," said a piping voice from the depths of an armchair that faced toward the window. A girl leaned around the chair back and grinned, a mischievous glint in her eyes. "Kashmira Jones, at your service."

She was wearing a deerstalker cap, and when she stood up to greet us, she took it off and long black hair tumbled down below her waist. She slapped the hat back on her head and took out a pipe which she cocked in our direction while squinting with one eye. "You have made a long journey across the ocean. It's not the usual time of year for exchange students, so you must be here on a mission. That one," she pointed at Ellen, "bites her nails and is determined to solve the case."

Ellen looked thunder at the mention of nails, but tilted her nose in the air when she talked about solving the case. "What if I am?"

"You," the girl said, pointing at Jayden, "have been in an accident."

"Obviously," Ellen said.

"With a giant."

"What do you know about it?" I asked.

"What's more, there have been grave robbers," Kashmira declared. She stuck the pipe in her mouth and glared at us.

"That's old news," Alfie said. "Everyone knows someone is stealing corpses from the local church."

I was so shocked I forgot about Kashmira's statement about the giant. I remembered the crumbling gray church in Chesterton with the crooked gravestones. Someone was digging up the graves?

"What do you call this?" She held up a test tube with a violet liquid. She didn't wait for us to answer. "It's proof that the thieves brought a body back to Camp Dickens. One of the Doyles spotted a tall stranger on the premises carrying something last night and followed him to the bog. This morning we found a hair at the site and tested it. The hair in this test tube matches the hair of one of the corpses."

"You're forgetting the missing quality," Alfie intoned, putting a finger alongside his nose. "Holmes taught that the facts are not enough. A good officer must have imagination. Stella?" He looked at me meaningfully.

"What?" I retorted. "I have no idea what this means."

"You disappoint me," Alfie said. "Clearly we need to see the scene of the crime for ourselves." He whipped a magnifying glass from a mahogany sideboard. "Let's go!"

Kashmira slumped back in her chair. "I've already been over the ground. You know my gift."

"What's her gift?" I whispered to Alfie.

"Finding clues," he answered, scowling. "But it doesn't hurt to go over the ground again."

I noticed that the table had a dozen other test tubes with violet liquid, but one of them was green. "What's the green one?"

"We're still trying to figure it out," Kashmira said.

❧❧

We walked behind the house with Alfie stooping over to study the ground with the magnifying glass. The Doyle dorm was at the top of the same steep slope we had navigated last night. If I'd seen it in daylight, I never would have tried to go down it in the dark.

Moulton stumped up the hill toward us with a large basket on his back, carrying brown shriveled strips of turf. He bent under the load and stopped to wipe his forehead with a handkerchief.

"Moulton collects the peat for the fires," Alfie explained.

Jayden swung toward him on his crutches. "Can I help?" he asked.

Moulton glared at him with a humph and walked past the group.

Alfie shrugged. "He doesn't like to be interfered with. He takes it as an insult."

Jayden gazed after the old man shuffling up the path, and I wondered if he was using levitation to help, despite the old man's hostility. Moulton seemed to straighten under the load, and his step quickened. Jayden watched him until the hunched figure turned a corner.

"Why doesn't he like us?" I asked.

"That's easy. Moulton doesn't like anybody," Alfie said.

"Has he been here long?"

"I just met him last week. He's a retired janitor from MI-7 and asked to be posted here. Even our support staff have to be insiders due to the top secret nature of camp."

We continued down the path, which was overgrown with rough grass and scrubby bushes. At the bottom of the hill Alfie stopped at the edge of a huge meadow covered with yellow plants. Shallow pools and muddy patches dotted the area.

"This is Harlowe Bog," he said, sweeping his arm in a wide arc.

Something furry and brown darted from a clump of grass.

"Is it a rat?" Lindsey asked, her voice squeaking. She wasn't fond of rats.

"A water vole."

I took a step to get a better look, and saw the ground rippling around the spot where the water vole disappeared. "How strange." I went to take another step, but Alfie pulled me back.

"No farther. That's a quaking bog, and you don't want to fool around. Watch." He threw a stick into the middle of the yellow plants, and it slowly sank.

I swallowed, and my hands grew clammy with sweat. "You let me take a step in that?"

"Don't you have bogs in the United States?" he asked, a teasing sparkle in his eyes.

I grabbed the magnifying glass from him and began studying the ground, trying to hide the blush burning on my cheeks.

"Wait, there's something there," Ellen said. "Something gold.

"Where?" Jayden asked.

Ellen pointed to a spot deep in the bog.

"It's not safe," Alfie said.

Jayden stared hard at the spot, and the mud began to burble, a thin log rising slowly from the ooze. It was covered with green slime, but flecks of gold showed through in patches. Jayden floated it toward us, and I realized it wasn't a log. Dangling from the bottom were five fingers, wrinkled and brown. A cold chill swept down my back. Lindsey screamed, and we ran.

We didn't stop till we were safely in the yard behind 221 Baker Street.

"What in the world was that?" Ellen demanded.

Alfie was so pale his lips had turned purple. "It must have been a bog body," he said, still breathing heavily. "They discover them from time to time—people from the Iron Age whose bodies have been mummified in the peat bog. The arm must have broken free when Moulton was cutting peat." He wiped the sweat from his forehead with his sleeve, and slowly the color returned to his face. "I've only seen them in the museum before this."

Jayden swung up on his crutches. "I put it back where it belongs," he said quietly. "Sorry about that."

"Not to worry. In our country we're digging up bodies all the time, especially when there's new construction."

"How awful," I said.

"We show proper respect for the bones, you know. Bury them again in a safe place. Some people think the bog was sacred ground for Iron Age people. That body was probably laid to rest with the gold sheath on the arm as part of a ritual."

"Sorry we didn't find any more clues for Kashmira," Lindsey said.

"Maybe we did," I said. "What if it wasn't an accident that the bog body floated up when Moulton was cutting peat? What if *he's* the one stealing corpses from the church graveyard?"

Alfie shuddered. "What would he want with just an arm?"

The afternoon was a Sudoku contest with the Doyles, but our team decided to take the day off. The shock of finding a piece of a bog body left us needing time for quiet. Ellen had finished *A Christmas Carol* but was in the middle of another Dickens book. I curled up in a window seat with *Treasure Island* to find out what happened next on the Hispaniola. Older kids on their way to the library or dorm rooms passed by, and in the distance I heard two people practicing for the insult contest and Moulton's dogs barking as he banged through the back door.

I'd just gotten to the part where Jim overheard Long John Silver plotting his evil plan when Downey called me to the kitchen for tea and biscuits. I was still lost in the story and barely said hello as she handed me the tray.

She cocked her head to the side. "You've got the look of your mother about you today," she said. "*Fey*, we used to call it. Fairy-like. As though she was looking right through you."

I blushed, the spell of the story breaking in an instant. "I'm sorry. I was reading and still thinking about the story."

She gave me one of her warm smiles. "Ah, the lure of a good book. You may take the tray along to your reading nook, Duckie."

I wasn't used to carrying a tray with hot tea and wished I had Jayden's gift of levitation as I wobbled back to my window seat. The book was where I left it, but a conker lay on top of it, anchoring a newspaper cutting that fluttered in the breeze from the open window.

The headline read "Eminent Scientist Seeks New Cure," and it was an interview with Dr. Bruce Jaeger! The reporter explained that the scientist's work dealt with how healing takes place among cells and might lead to an entirely new view of medicine in the future. He quoted Jaeger telling how he was inspired as a child when an experimental procedure for bone marrow transplant saved his life.

My mind flew to his big brother Buckeye, our head counselor at camp, who traveled through time to donate that bone marrow. I wondered if Bruce ever knew that

"Uncle Buckeye" was really his big brother arrived from the future.

The article ended with an interesting statement. "I am dedicating my research to a group of four young people from the United States..." and he listed our names. Was that why MI-7 wanted us here? Did they think we had some kind of inside information about Bruce Jaeger? And why did he dedicate his research to us? Did he know we had helped his brother?

I held the glossy conker in the palm of my hand. Why did these keep turning up?

≈≈

CHAPTER NINE

≈≈

I found Ellen just before dinner, her face red from crying. "I'm never reading anything by Dickens again. His stories are too tragic."

"What did you read?" I asked.

My question set off another bout of tears, but she held up the book—*A Tale of Two Cities*.

"He dies in the end!" she choked out. "Sacrifices his life and says *it's a far, far better thing he does—*"

"Wait, are you saying that's the meaning of our Team Dickens T-shirts?"

She nodded while the tears ran down her cheeks. "And then he says *it's a far, far better rest he goes to than he has ever known.*"

I wasn't sure this was the right motto for a team, but perhaps I needed to read the book for myself.

Lindsey joined us, starry-eyed and cradling a small blue book labeled *Classic Poems*. "This is the best book ever," she announced. "I'm bringing it with us to the evening activity. Alfie says we're having a poetry reading at the Tennyson dorm."

I thought Ellen would re-shelf the detested *Tale of Two Cities*, but I caught her hiding it under her pillow before we left. She stuck her chin in the air. "I might have to read the ending again," she said.

The Tennysons lived in a mansion even grander than Gad's Hill Place. Alfie told us it was called Farringford House and was a replica of Lord Tennyson's home on the Isle of Wight. He took us around the ivy-covered walls to the back, where arched windows and interesting projections jumbled together. There was even a turret on one side.

Lindsey stopped under an ancient tree and spread her arms wide. "Immemorial elms, and murmuring of innumerable bees," she said, her voice soft and smooth.

"What are you talking about?" I asked.

"It's from a poem by Tennyson. I read it today, and I like those lines. Can you hear them?"

"Hear what?"

"The bees."

I listened, and a low hum seemed to come from the flower beds.

"The poetry reading is over here," Alfie called. He seemed nervous tonight and kept looking at his watch.

He led us to a corner of the garden where chairs had been set in rows near tall green hedges that separated the lawn from the forest that surrounded it. On one side was an arbor that still had clusters of grapes on the vine, now shriveled into raisins, and on the other side was an old gazebo. The roof sloped steeply with fanciful swirls made of iron at the peak. It had no walls, and roses grew up the four columns at the corners. A few late roses still bloomed, their sweet scent reminding me of Grandma and home.

"This must be lovely in summer," Lindsey said.

"It is," Alfie replied. He plucked a rose from the gazebo and presented it with a bow to me. I hesitated and felt my cheeks flaming red.

"Th-thank you," I stuttered. I was mortified—here I was in the land of Jane Austen and I couldn't even accept a flower gracefully.

"Excuse me. I must leave you." Without another word, he jogged back across the lawn.

"I noticed he didn't give roses to the rest of us," Ellen said, her mouth curving in a lopsided smile.

"Not another word," I said.

Kashmira Jones was passing out slips of paper. "Take one if you'd like to recite a poem," she said, pressing one into my hands.

"I didn't come prepared." I tried to hand it back, but Lindsey snatched it from me.

"I'll take it." She tugged me away from the others and showed me the piece of paper. Below the number *11*, was a penciled message: *Meet me behind the grape arbor after the reading.* Lindsey raised her eyebrows in a perfect imitation of Alfie, and we giggled.

"You tell the others," she said, waving the poetry book at me. "I'm going to pick out a poem and make sure I've got all the words."

I thought I wouldn't be able to concentrate on the poetry after Kashmira's mysterious message, but the poems pulled me in. Our chairs faced the gazebo, and the campers stood on the top step to recite the poems.

One of the Stevensons had the first number and opened with a short poem by their founder that had lovely words like: *the golden smell of broom* and *the shade of pine.*

Most of the Stevenson poems were quick like that one, and many of the kids had their poems memorized. But the Tennyson poems were long, and the campers read them with a book light that Kashmira gave them since the evening was growing darker. There was a lovely poem about the Arabian Nights and one about a sailor boy who whistled to the morning star. One kid read *The Charge of the Light Brigade* in a stirring voice:

> *Theirs not to reason why,*
> *Theirs but to do and die.*
> *Into the valley of Death*
> *Rode the Six Hundred.*

Jayden and the cricket team stood up and cheered at the end.

Kashmira Jones recited a piece by Sir Arthur Conan Doyle about hunting, and it captured the feeling of autumn perfectly—*red leaves flying* and *red bracken dying.*

Lindsey's number eleven was the last of the bunch. She read a Tennyson poem about Sir Galahad. I could see why she liked it. There was a line:

> *My strength is as the strength of ten*

Because my heart is pure.

It told the story of a knight who saw a holy vision. That sounded like Lindsey too. Part way through the poem, I thought I heard a sigh from the tall hedge surrounding our poetry space. It almost sounded like a cow lowing, and I wondered if there were cattle grazing nearby. The sun had almost set, and it was hard to see Lindsey standing in the gazebo—just the twinkle of the book light—but her voice carried clearly:

My spirit beats her mortal bars,
As down dark tides the glory slides,
And star-like mingles with the stars.

A deep groan came from the bushes, and Jayden tapped my arm. He heard it too.

"I'm going to investigate," I whispered.

In the dusk it was easy to slip away. I crept warily toward the hedge, only half-listening to the poem.

Lindsey continued:

I yearn to breathe the airs of heaven
That often meet me here.
I muse on joy that will not cease,
Pure spaces clothed in living beams,
Pure lilies of eternal peace,
Whose odours haunt my dreams—

At that point a wail of pain came from the bushes, and I forgot my caution. I plunged through the greenery, expecting to see someone in danger, but no one was there.

Jayden pushed through the hedge behind me. He had ditched his crutches and was limping.

"What are you doing without crutches?" I hissed.

"Look!" He pointed to the shadows where a huge figure walked quickly, dragging one foot, which rasped over the fallen leaves. Jayden pulled me back into the shrubbery. "Don't let him see us," he whispered.

The giant reached a patch of moonlight, and I saw that his head was shaved on one side and a long row of black stitches ran across the top. My gut swirled and my dinner threatened to come back up.

He raised his head and sniffed the air, then turned directly toward us. He couldn't possibly see us in our hiding place, but my skin crawled like a thousand ants were swarming over my skin. His stare was glassy, vacant.

He tilted his face toward the moon and howled a weird cry—a long series of half words. The night sounds in the woods hushed for a moment, and I held my breath, clenching sweaty palms against my chest as though I could quiet my heart. It beat so loudly I feared it would give away our position.

The last of the eerie cry ended on a strangled note, and the creature stepped into the gloom and disappeared among the trees. We didn't move until the sound of his scraping footstep had completely died out. Even then, I wasn't sure I could trust myself to walk.

"That's the guy I chased last night," Jayden said.

I shivered. "He's like something out of a nightmare."

The bushes rustled, and Kashmira with her flashlight squeezed in. "Did you see him?" she asked, her voice urgent. "We were waiting behind the arbor, but you never came."

Lindsey and Ellen were right behind her. "Who was it?" Ellen asked.

Kashmira shrugged. "That's why I wanted to confer with you. I've seen him three times—always at night, and always on the fringes watching us." She turned on Jayden. "You chased him last night. Who do you think he is? Or what?" She said the last words slowly, menacingly.

Jayden shook his head like he thought she was crazy. "There has to be a logical explanation. Is there a hospital near here?"

"Nothing for miles," she replied. "That's what makes this an excellent mystery."

"Did you tell Downey?" I asked.

Kashmira shined the flashlight directly in my eyes. "Are you crazy? This is a Doyle mystery—I'm only sharing it with you because you're outsiders. Even Alfie doesn't know." She played the light around our circle. "Besides, I think you may be the key to the mystery. The monster appeared the same day you did."

I looked at Jayden, and I could tell he was thinking the same thing I was. If the monster was the one we were trying to draw out, Alfie would never let us pursue him on our own.

Kashmira clicked off the flashlight and her voice came ghostly in the darkness. "You must tell no one."

"We won't," I said.

ૐ৵

CHAPTER TEN

ૐ৵

A chilly rain set in as we walked home, and we woke the next morning to find the first frost had fallen. The lawn around Gad's Hill Place sparkled like ice. Lindsey and I wrapped ourselves in our warmest coats and returned to the Tennyson dorm to find the poetry book. She had left it in the gazebo, but it wasn't there.

"I put it *here* on the railing," she insisted.

"Perhaps it fell in the grass." I walked around the structure to the place she pointed, but instead of a poetry book, a huge footprint was pressed in the earth. There was only one person who could make a print that big. "We need to show this to Kashmira."

"Irene!" piped a voice from the bushes. "Did you call?" A boy popped up, and I recognized him as one of the Doyles I danced with at the ball. "I can get Kashmira for you."

He dashed off before I could thank him.

"Did he just call you *Irene*?" Lindsey asked.

"I think it's my new nickname," I said. I didn't want to rehash my exploits dashing through the lines of dancers at the ball. "I think it has something to do with Sherlock Holmes."

Kashmira brought a suitcase of chemicals and whipped up a thick plaster mixture to take an impression of the footprint. "This is going to crack the case wide open," she said, smoothing the plaster until it looked like cake icing.

"How?"

"The grave robber brought the body here, and if this footprint belongs to him, it's proof he's hanging about."

"Do we tell the police?"

"No." She scowled. "We don't tell anyone, not even Alfie and Downey. This is our case, and we're going to unravel the mystery ourselves."

"What if it's just a camp prank?" I asked.

She squinted at me. "I wouldn't put it past the Stevensons."

She put the hardened plaster imprint in her suitcase and snapped it shut. "The game's afoot. Pun intended." Then she slapped her deerstalker cap on her head and melted into the bushes.

❧

Lunch was leek and potato soup, which sounded funny but tasted delicious. The leeks were sharp as onions, and the potatoes melted into the creamy white broth. I held the bowl in my hands to warm them while I listened to the wind wuthering in the chimney.

"Do you think it's odd we don't have classes like at Camp Hawthorne?" Ellen asked.

"That's because you're here off-season," Alfie said. "Serving as bait." He had come up quietly behind us, and I startled.

"Where were you last night?" I asked. "We waited for you in the parlor but you never got back."

He seemed pleased that I wanted to know. "Babysitting for a friend of Downey," he said, but he didn't give any details. "We're going on a nature walk this afternoon, so dress warmly. I'm to give you these." He passed around pocket-size sketchbooks and boxes of colored pencils.

Jayden levitated the pencils in a swirly pattern in front of his face. "What are we supposed to do with them?"

"You're going to sketch pictures of the plants we find."

"Brilliant," Lindsey said.

"Rats," said Ellen at the same time. "I can't draw at all."

"You could explore underground on our hike," I teased.

"Underground might be easier to draw," she replied.

Jayden no longer needed his crutches. He still had a bandage on his leg, but he assured us it was completely healed. He even sprinted around the house a few times when Downey wasn't looking. "Man, it feels good to run again," he said.

Downey led the nature expedition. Though the day was chilly, the sun was bright. She wore a wide-brimmed straw hat with a gauzy scarf tied around the top and under her chin.

"Every well-educated young lady learned to draw in Mr. Dickens's day," she said, her high voice carrying to the back of the group.

Campers from other dorms had joined us. Oliver was there, too, which made me wonder if he ever got around to research. Lindsey edged closer to his group, but I pulled her back toward the front of the line. "You don't want to miss any of this," I said.

We hiked a long way behind Gad's Hill Place to the ruins of a little chapel. A single arched window remained, set high in the wall, though the glass was gone. The other three sides rose only a few feet above my head, enclosing a plot of grass with scattered paving stones. The roof was open to the sky, and vines and wild flowers grew over the crumbling walls.

"The greenery is wall spleenwort," Downey trilled. "And the purple bell-shaped flowers in the crevices are harebells." She plucked one of the purple flowers and passed it to me. "The girls in your mother's day used to press these in a book for keepsakes."

I looked wonderingly at the tiny flower in my hand. Had my mother saved one of these long ago? I breathed in the crisp autumn air, feeling close to her even in this faraway place.

"What are those cottony flowers?" Lindsey asked, pointing to a cluster of plants growing in the grass beside the chapel.

"Thistles, and the fluffy white part is the seed. The goldfinches love them—see?" She pointed farther afield where a small brown bird with yellow wing tips and red markings, perched on a thistle. He was so beautiful—the yellow and red glowing like jewels—that time seemed to stop for a moment. Then Oliver bumbled toward it, and the tiny creature flew away.

"Ooh, I missed him," Lindsey said. She had already whipped out her pencil and sketched the bird's outline in her notebook.

"That's very good, dear." Downey peered through her spectacles at the sketch. "Did you know the Anglo-Saxon name for the bird was thistle-tweaker? And a flock is called a *charm* of goldfinches. Rather quaint, isn't it?" She opened a portable chair and sat down. "We will stop here to draw for a few minutes."

"Let's go where it's quieter," I said in an undertone. The Austens continued to wade through the grass and thistles, laughing and joking and scaring away the wildlife.

We walked to the other side of the ruined chapel, and Lindsey found another thistle to draw. She cleverly sketched it so that the bird appeared to be eating the seeds, with bits of the downy thistle floating above his head.

I made my sketch scientific—a picture of just the leaf, then a sketch of the thistle head with seeds, and one of a single seed. It looked like an illustration in a science textbook, and I was pleased with it. I got out my purple pencil to try the harebells next. Some of them were growing next to a creek at the bottom of the hill. I walked toward them but never got to make my sketch. In the soft mud, a huge footprint pointed straight into the creek.

My pulse racing, I quickly crossed the trickle of water by jumping from stone to stone. Another footprint was planted on the far bank, aimed into the woods. I looked back at the others. Lindsey was bent over her sketchbook, and Ellen with two sticks was leading Jayden around. It would only take a minute to follow the trail since the tracks would probably disappear among the fallen leaves.

I scouted the area for the next print and almost missed it—it was at least five feet beyond the first one. By following the line between the two, I found another impression, but it was just the toe mark. I bent to study it and heard someone calling my name.

Ellen had crossed the creek and was walking toward me with her sticks quivering in front of her. "A huge underground waterway used to run along here," she began. "It's dried up, but there are tons of artifacts like helmets, bowls, silver coins." She stopped abruptly. "That's odd. It's gone."

Alfie was waving his hands from the opposite bank and beckoning for us to return.

"Lover boy's looking for you," she teased. "Too bad—this was just getting fun."

I ignored her comment and pointed to the tracks. Her eyebrows shot up at the sight of them. "Our mysterious giant was here."

ري ين

CHAPTER ELEVEN

ري ين

After the sun went down Alfie dropped us off at the Stevenson island.

"Toolaroo," he said. "Downey has another job for me."

"Somehow I can't see a big MI-7 guy babysitting," I said.

Alfie's ears turned red. "It's actually a top-secret mission," he said and stalked away.

Ellen nudged me with her shoulder. "He's trying so hard to impress you, Stella. Can't you give him a break?"

"Why would I do that?" I said, but inside I was wondering if she was right. Was that why Alfie stayed so close at the beginning? Perhaps I'd hurt his feelings and now he was avoiding me.

The Stevensons were hosting a huge game of *Dr. Jekyll and Mr. Hyde*. It was like tag, and *Mr. Hyde* tried to catch everyone. If you got tagged, you turned into another *Mr. Hyde*, and helped chase the rest of the *Dr. Jekylls*. The last person standing would win. We used the entire island and carried flashlights since it was growing dark. The Austens were particularly devious. They would hide in the bushes and jump out when you least expected it, or they would pretend to be on your side and then grab you at the last minute and reveal they were really Mr. Hyde.

The younger Doyle boys also had the unnerving habit of popping out at odd times. They would tip an imaginary hat at me and shout "Irene!" but they never tried to tag me. I definitely needed to read more Sherlock Holmes stories.

Jayden and Oliver were the last two free people, and the entire pack of Mr. Hydes, screaming like banshees, pursued them around and around the house. I cut back and ran the other way, but Amelia had the same idea. She caught Jayden before I could catch Oliver, and the Austens won.

The Stevensons presented Oliver with a crown woven from palm fronds and invited everyone inside for brownies and coconut milk.

"Where's Lindsey?" I asked the others as we waited in the food line.

"Wasn't she tagged about the same time you were?" Ellen asked.

"Yeah, she took off after one of the Austens who was trying to cheat and cross the bridge," I said.

Oliver was right behind us, looking rakish again with his palm crown tilted to the side. "That was me, but I swerved around and lost her. I think she kept running over the bridge." He smiled a jaunty smile, and I turned my back on him.

"If she kept going, something could have happened to her," I muttered to the others.

"We better investigate," Jayden said.

The bridge by flashlight was creepy. I felt every tremor and sway, and our lights reflected eerily from the scum on the black water. I called Lindsey's name but the only sound was the creaking of the bridge and an occasional hoot from an owl.

Suddenly, a chorus of barking erupted from the chestnut woods. We ran toward the sound as the barking and growling grew louder and more vicious, and then I heard Lindsey scream. We burst into a clearing where she stood, her back against a tree, wildly swinging her flashlight at two dogs that were leaping for her face.

"Scram!" yelled Jayden, charging at them.

They turned and snarled at him, but a gruff voice cut them off. "That'll do. Down, girls."

Moulton hobbled toward us with the old dog, Henry, at his side. He carried a powerful flashlight, which he shone on Lindsey and the two dogs, now sitting obediently at her feet. "You all right, lassie?"

"I'm fine," she said, but her voice was quivery.

"Best get on home," he said. "These woods aren't safe at night."

Henry had drifted over to me and now sat looking up at me with pleading eyes. "How are you, old boy," I said, rubbing the rough fur along his back. He whimpered and lay down. "Is he hurt?" I asked.

"Just old," Moulton said. He whistled softly to Henry, but he didn't move. Then Moulton did an amazing thing. He stooped and picked him up—unusual strength for an old man.

"Can I help you, sir?" Jayden asked.

Moulton staggered. "Thank you, son."

Jayden floated Henry gently in the air a few inches in front of Moulton, while the old man kept his hand on the dog's head. The other two trotted at his heels.

Ellen and I went to help Lindsey, but she waved us off. "I'll be fine in a minute," she said. "Just need to get over the fright."

"What happened?"

"I'll tell you when we get back to the dorm."

When we reached the dorm, Alfie still wasn't back, and we couldn't find Downey either. I was disappointed—I'd become accustomed to gathering little tidbits from her about my parents, and I missed her when she was absent.

Ellen made us cups of hot cocoa while Jayden helped Moulton to the gamekeeper's lodge behind the main house. We found sugar cookies on a plate and took them with the cocoa to the parlor. Lindsey began to shiver, and I wrapped her in a blanket and made her sit by the glowing peat fire.

Jayden, frowning, joined us. "I'm worried about Moulton. He looks like he's going to crack. Wanted me to put Henry on his lap, and when I left he was just sitting there with tears running down his face."

"Henry's old," I said. "He's afraid of losing him."

"But he must be used to losing dogs by now. Look how many he has."

"It never gets easy," Ellen said.

Lindsey wrapped her blanket tight around herself. "It's more than that. I got a confused message from his brain, and he's scared because Henry's death means something more."

"How did you end up in the woods?" I asked.

The color had returned to Lindsey's cheeks, and she laughed. "It was stupid really. I saw Oliver running over the bridge and chased him."

"What a coincidence that you chased Oliver," Ellen said, curling the L so it sounded like *Olley-ver*.

"You have to admit he's smashing," she said.

"Yuck!" Ellen said.

Lindsey's chin went up. "At any rate, he was too fast. I thought I lost him, but then I heard someone running ahead of me on the bridge. You know how it creaks. I chased after him, and he crashed into the woods, which are bigger than you might think. We ran so long, I realized I'd better catch him or I'd never find my way out. Then my flashlight burned out. I started calling Oliver's name and telling him I needed help, but he was gone. So I reached out toward his mind, and it wasn't Oliver."

Lindsey shivered and took a sip of hot cocoa. "He told me his name was Peter, and he lived in the woods. He can't talk—something wrong with his tongue—and he has no friends. He was watching our game when I started chasing him. I told him I was lost, and he said he'd lead me back, but I mustn't try to see him. I heard the sound of rustling leading me back the way I came, and I followed it a pretty good distance, but suddenly Moulton's dogs started barking. I thought they were going to attack me, and I screamed, and you arrived."

"Did you see who was helping you?" I asked.

Lindsey cradled the warm cocoa in her hands. "No, but I think I know—he's someone who's been watching on the fringes."

"The monster?" Ellen said, choking on her cocoa.

"Don't call him that," Lindsey said.

"Should we tell Alfie?" I asked. "Maybe the big guy is the one we're supposed to draw out of hiding?"

"His name is Peter," Lindsey said. She looked like she was going to cry, but Jayden didn't seem to notice.

"No," he said. "Alfie doesn't want us solving this on our own. We'll let him think we're acting as bait like he wants, but we'll figure this out ourselves."

Lindsey seemed on the verge of a breakdown so I didn't stick around for the rest of the talk. I walked with her back to our dorm room. She still had the blanket wrapped around her, and her blonde hair was tangled with leaves from the evening adventure.

She laid a hand on my arm to stop me before we reached the room. "I didn't mention this to the others, but Peter promised to talk to me again when he could. He really isn't a monster."

I just hoped Lindsey was right.

ৼৡৡ

CHAPTER TWELVE

ৼৡৡ

Alfie was definitely avoiding me at breakfast, and I felt bad for teasing him about babysitting. If Ellen was right and he had a crush on me, I needed to figure out a way to let him down easy. I asked Lindsey for advice, and she promised to consult her beloved Jane Austen books for ideas.

Kashmira was waiting for us at breakfast. "I've come to pick up Jayden for the cricket game," she said, "But I have another clue for you as well."

I buttered one of Downey's delicious scones and savored the first bite. I was only half listening.

"Do you remember the hair we found at the bog that proved the grave robbers were bringing the bodies here?" she asked.

I remembered the violet test tubes and the odd green one. "There was a second hair you couldn't identify," I said.

Kashmira smiled at me like I was a good student who had answered correctly. "I finally figured out the source—it's from a black dog, probably one of Moulton's. Now what do you deduce from that?"

I forgot about the scone and let the possibilities brim in my mind. They weren't real possibilities because lately I only got the snarling dogs when I tried to use my gift. "Do you think Moulton is the thief?"

"Perhaps in cahoots with the monster."

"We're not to call him that anymore," Ellen said. She told Kashmira the whole story from last night, and I had the satisfaction of seeing her so surprised that she had to take out her pipe and bite down on the stem—hard.

"They're working together and that's why the ...er... big guy doesn't want anyone to see his face. He's probably the strong man and Moulton is the brains," Kashmira said.

"Do we tell Downey now?" I asked.

She squinted at me. "Can you imagine the mess she would make of this? She means well, but she'd give the whole thing away. No, we have to make our own trap so we can present the authorities with a tidy solution."

Lindsey refused to believe that Peter was the grave robber, but she agreed to help us find him. She told Kashmira about the way she communicated with him by thought transference.

"Smashing!" she replied.

Kashmira left with Jayden for the cricket match, and the others prepared to watch the Shakespeare Insult Contest, but I had a better plan. "Downey's judging the contest, right? This is our perfect chance to read those off-limits books in the library."

"But I was going to cheer for Oliver in the contest," Lindsey said.

I rolled my eyes. "You've got to give up on him. Buckeye's little brother is in danger, and we're no closer to drawing out the bad guys. We need to push harder to crack this case."

I realized I was sounding like Kashmira, and I stopped abruptly.

Lindsey twirled her hair into a bun and stuck a pencil in it—her version of a no-nonsense attitude. "Let's do this!"

We started with the books in the MI-7 section of the library, each of us taking one and scanning the table of contents for something important. Unfortunately, everything seemed to involve people from a hundred years ago.

"These books are as dull as door nails," Ellen said. She reached for another one, but it seemed to stick to the shelf. She gave it a tug, and an entire section of wall swung outward with a click. "A secret passage!" she said, her voice sharp with excitement.

"I'll stand guard," Lindsey said quickly. She didn't like closed-in spaces.

I went first, and there was just enough room to slide sideways along the wall. The air was thick with dust, and I sneezed.

Ellen slipped in next to me.

"Are you sure it's safe?" Lindsey's anxious voice drifted through the opening.

"We're fine—just close the door behind us and put the books back in case someone comes," I said.

"I hope there aren't spiders here," Ellen intoned in the gloom.

"Don't worry. I've got a flashlight if we need it." But I hoped we wouldn't. Exploring secret passages in the dark was on the top of my list of exciting projects.

Once the door closed, the darkness was complete except for pinpricks of light every few feet. I put my eyes to one and saw the library, lined with shelves, and Lindsey putting back the books we had removed. I slithered farther along the passage with my right arm feeling for a wall, and to my surprise the passage opened into a wider space. My hand brushed against a string, too heavy for a spider web. I pulled on it and a single light bulb sprang to life. The space was about the size of a closet and had a desk and wooden chair. A glossy brown nut rested on top of a piece of paper on the desk.

"A conker again!" Ellen said.

I picked up the nut and rolled it around the palm of my hand. "Whoever is leaving these must use this passage. That's how they snuck in and flipped those pages in the MI-7 book."

The paper was blank except for a few words: "Life Force—permanent or temporary?"

"What does it mean?" Ellen asked.

I closed my eyes and reached out for a possibility. At first I thought I might get something. I had a glimpse of Moulton with Henry, but then the image returned to the snarling dogs jumping at the gate, and I shuddered. "I can't get a reading on it."

"Oliver, how nice to see you!" Lindsey's voice came loud and clear from the direction of the library.

Ellen motioned me back to the passage, and we looked through the peepholes. Lindsey was smiling and asking Oliver about the Shakespeare Insult Competition. He didn't seem his usual rakish self and grumbled that the judges weren't fair this year. Lindsey sat on a table, swinging her legs. "How about your research?" she asked brightly.

"It's a dead end," he said glumly. "I thought I'd find more about the life force that Dr. Mesmer discovered, but all the research on the subject has disappeared from the library."

"What's the life force?" she asked.

"Mesmer thought it was an energy that could transfer between living things, even restore life to a dead body."

At that moment Alfie stuck his head through the library door. "Ah Lindsey, just the person I wanted to see. Do you know where Stella is?"

Ellen tapped my elbow in the dark and gasped like she was trying not to giggle.

What do I say? Lindsey's panicked question burst into my mind.

Tell him I was going with Ellen to the Swiss chalet, I sent back the thought.

She relayed my message, and Alfie seemed pleased. "Don't tell her, but I'm planning a surprise picnic." He paused and looked back and forth between Lindsey and Oliver. "You two are invited as well."

"Brilliant," cooed Lindsey. "You boys go ahead. I just have to find a book before I leave." She wandered over to the Jane Austen section, but as soon as they left, she ran to the MI-7 bookshelf and activated the door to the passage. "Stella and Ellen, are you there?" she whispered. We promptly appeared in the doorway, and she jumped.

"Quick, close it back up for us," I said. "Ellen and I are going to run overland and beat them there."

Through the window I saw Oliver's head disappearing down the tunnel to the Swiss chalet. Ellen and I sprinted across the lawn and over the street that separated the house from the chalet, then through the bushes and arrived breathless just as Alfie bobbed up from the tunnel. We sat down with our backs to him and pretended we were blowing thistle seeds for fun.

"American girls are different," I heard Alfie saying in his authoritative voice, but he broke off when I turned and waved.

"What a nice surprise. How are you Alfie?"

He flicked his black hair out of his eyes and raised his eyebrows. "Cheerio!" Then he seemed to be stuck for a moment, and a red blush crept up his neck.

Ellen was eying him critically. "I just figured out who you look like," she said. "Your hair is like the Beatles."

Alfie ran a hand through his hair, which was hard to do while holding a picnic basket with the other one. "Some people say I look like John Lennon." He set down the basket and put on a pair of wire rim glasses he carried in his pocket. "What do you think?"

"Brilliant!" Oliver said.

Ellen nudged me with her foot. "Yeah, like twins," I said. I didn't really know anything about John Lennon, but we needed to humor Alfie.

I signaled Ellen for help, making my eyes as wide as possible, and she took over. "I like his song *All you Need is Love.*" She hummed a few bars and Oliver joined in. He had a pretty good voice.

At that moment Lindsey showed up waving some napkins at us. "Downey sent me with these—said she forgot to put them in the basket."

Alfie suddenly remembered the picnic basket. "I thought you all might like some lunch," he said.

"Smashing idea," Ellen gushed, looking meaningfully at me.

"Yeah, smashing," I echoed.

The meal was amazing—egg salad sandwiches, fizzy bottles of elderberry soda, juicy dill pickles and a type of biscuit I'd never tried before with bits of orange cheese inside it.

Alfie kept the wire rim glasses on throughout the meal, shooting nervous glances at me from time to time. I smiled and pretended not to notice how strange he was acting. It was a relief when he said he had to leave. Oliver went with him.

"What did I tell you?" Ellen crowed triumphantly as they disappeared down the tunnel. "He's smitten all right."

I groaned. I had enough problems without trying to figure out how to deal with Alfie.

≈✑≈

CHAPTER THIRTEEN

≈✑≈

Lindsey wanted to explore the Swiss chalet after lunch, so we climbed the stairs to the second floor. The tiny room had a simple writing desk with drawers full of paper and pens. There was even one fountain pen with an ink bottle. "You don't suppose this belonged to Charles Dickens?" she asked, staring at the pen in a dreamy way.

She plopped down at the desk and unscrewed the lid from the bottle of ink. "I'm going to write something at his desk with this pen."

"It would be hard to come up with a story more amazing than the one we're living now," I said. I told Lindsey about the secret room and the paper with *life force* on it.

"Isn't it strange that Oliver is researching the same thing?" Ellen asked.

"Do you think he's the mole?" I said.

"He does keep popping up—even went on the nature walk with us."

"But why would he hide his own research?" Lindsey said. Her attempt at writing with pen and ink had degenerated to a doodle with spirals and ink blots.

"Maybe it's his excuse for poking around."

"Halloo!" called a voice from down below. "Permission to come aboard?"

I stuck my head out the window and waved to Kashmira, who had arrived with her sleuthing suitcase. "I looked all over for you after the cricket match," she said. "Oliver told me you were here."

Ellen giggled. "Yeah, having a romantic picnic with Alfie and Olly-ver."

"Did you save me anything? I'm famished."

"I still have one of Downey's cheese biscuits," I said.

Kashmira wolfed it down, talking at the same time. "You should have been there for the cricket match. Jayden was brilliant. The Doyles lost, but the Dickens are going into the final tournament this afternoon." She paused and studied my face. "I'm surprised Alfie didn't tell you about it. He's on the team, but of course he wasn't as brilliant as Jayden."

She clicked open her suitcase, and brought out a small notebook wrapped with a rubber band. "I came for you because it's time to track down our grave robber giant."

"He's not the robber," Lindsey said.

"Okay, the big guy then. I've gone over my case book, and he seems to appear in the early evening. Today we're going to be ready for him."

"How are we going to do that?" I asked.

"Lindsey will try to make contact using thought transference, and when she does we're going to ask him to meet us." She looked around our circle, everyone registering different reactions. I was doubtful it would work, Lindsey obviously hoped for a meeting, and Ellen squinted warily.

"What do we do if he agrees to meet?" she asked.

"Leave that to me," Kashmira said, patting her suitcase confidently.

Since we had to wait anyway, we spent the rest of the afternoon watching the cricket finals. The Stevensons squared off against the Dickens, and Kashmira was right—Jayden was amazing. She explained the plays to us, pointing out where smart tactics made the difference. It was an exciting game, a lot like baseball, though it went on for hours.

"How much longer?" Ellen asked when the Stevensons were finally having their turn at bat after a long run by the Dickens.

"A typical match is six hours," Kashmira said.

"Whoa," Ellen said. "And I thought baseball was long."

"Unlike baseball, we have a tea break," she said with a smug smile.

The younger boys from the Doyle house sat in a huddle near us. I recognized many of them from the vintage ball. When they thought I wasn't looking, they jerked their head in my direction and made mysterious hand signs to one another. Several times I caught the word "Irene" hissed among them.

Kashmira kept frowning at them and shaking her head.

"What's up with them?" I finally asked.

She rolled her eyes. "I call them the Baker Street Irregulars. They've gotten it in their heads that you're Irene, and they can't decide if they should spy on you or run away screaming."

"Why?"

"Sherlock Holmes called Irene Adler *the* woman—the only one who ever pulled one over on him."

"Is it a compliment, then?"

"Sort of—she might have been on the wrong side of the law at the time. Of course, that's just conjecture. They're also obsessed with your locket."

"My locket?" I felt for the chain around my neck and pulled out the gold case.

"Something pretty special in there?" Kashmira asked with a wry smile.

"Yeah, I guess there is." I didn't want to say anymore, and she didn't ask me to explain. That was one of Kashmira's nicer features. Of course, she probably already had a theory of her own.

The sun was just beginning to set with more of the cricket game to go when Lindsey gasped. "Peter's here." We gathered around her. "He says he can only communicate when it's safe."

"What does that mean?" Ellen said, but Kashmira shushed her.

"And he thanks me for the poetry book. He says it makes his heart hurt."

"What poetry book?"

Lindsey blushed. "I think he believes I left my poetry book for him the night of the reading."

"Ask him if he will meet us," Kashmira said.

Lindsey paused for a moment, her head tilted to the side. "He says he will meet us by the ruined chapel, but he will be hidden. We mustn't try to see him."

Kashmira pulled me aside and opened her suitcase. "This is a taser," she said. "We're going to catch the grave robber."

My breath caught in my throat—I remembered the grisly giant I'd seen in the moonlight, and I wasn't sure this was a good idea.

"Don't tell the others," she whispered.

Lindsey was still narrating. "There's a goldfinch nest in a tree near the north wall, and he wants us to wait near it. He calls them goldie birds," she added, with an indulgent smile.

I was beginning to see why Lindsey had become fond of Peter. He was like a big kid. "Does he have a name for you?" I asked.

"Pure heart," she said. "From the poem I read when he was hiding in the bushes."

We started off at once, Lindsey humming and relaying Peter's thoughts from time to time. He had a chill today, and someone gave him a hat. He talked about the goldie bird he was going to visit and the woods where he lived. "He says it's like poetry: *the red leaves flying and the red bracken dying,*" she narrated.

"That's from the poem I read," Kashmira said, and her hand checked the clasp of her suitcase.

We had almost reached the hill with the ruined chapel, when a chorus of barking erupted behind us.

"Dash it all!" Kashmira said. "Moulton's dogs are going to ruin everything."

The barking grew louder and Lindsey shuddered. "Should I tell Peter?"

"He must hear them already."

We started running for the chapel, and the yapping and snarling grew so loud, Lindsey had to cover her ears to hear Peter's thoughts. "He ran away from the dogs, but he left a present on the wall."

By this time, the dogs were sprinting toward us yelping like crazy.

"Everyone up," Ellen commanded.

I scrambled up the crumbling wall, using vines for handholds, and perched on the top. Nearby, lay a red knitted cap with a delicate nest resting on it. It was made of slender twigs and lined with thistle down. A piece of a speckled egg shell still clung to the bottom.

Lindsey swung up beside me. "Isn't it lovely? He says the goldie birds were gone, and the nest was on the ground. It made him sad."

The snarling dogs cut off her words. They were jumping and growling at us, but they couldn't reach us.

I wondered impatiently where Moulton was. He shouldn't send out his attack dogs and not supervise them. The two dogs tried to outdo one another with leaping higher, and one of them bit the vine just below my foot and tore it away.

My anger boiled over like one of Downey's kettles. If Moulton couldn't be here, I'd have to do his job. "That'll do," I yelled, making my voice as stern as possible. "Down, girls."

It worked! They sat at the foot of the wall and stared up at me with their tongues hanging out, panting lazily.

Kashmira was studying the nest with a magnifying glass. She carefully packed it in her sleuthing suitcase and turned the magnifying glass on the knitted cap. "Lovely! There's a hair stuck inside—short hair like the giant has." She whipped out a pair of tweezers and gently transferred the hair to a plastic bag. Then she snapped the suitcase closed with the hat and bag inside.

Moulton hobbled up soon after, wiping his face. He stooped to pat the two dogs and then frowned up at us. "What have you lassies gotten yourself into?" he said.

Ellen tossed her red hair. "Nothing. We were hiking and your dogs attacked us."

"Did they now? Don't usually attack without they're after something."

"Where's Henry?" I asked.

"Not well at all," he said, the gruffness leaking out of him. "Not well at all." He whistled to his dogs and they trotted behind him as he slowly walked away.

Kashmira stuck her pipe in her mouth. "He's not his usual crusty self today. Something's wrong."

"Perhaps he knows we're onto him," I said. "He kept us from trapping his partner."

Lindsey was picking harebells from the crevices of the wall. "Peter's not his partner," she said. "He's scared of the dogs."

Kashmira climbed down from the wall, hugging her suitcase with one arm. "Interesting observation. I'll let you know what I find once I process the clues."

❧❧

Chapter Fourteen

❧❧

After our adventure we were late for dinner, and Downey fussed at us. "You can't be traipsing all over the place when there are regular meals."

"We're sorry," Ellen said. "But the picnic you made was so good we forgot about eating."

Downey smiled at the compliment and gave us extra large servings of some yellow fluffy stuff. "It's neeps and tatties," she said. "Americans would call them mashed turnips and potatoes."

"How about the meat?" Ellen asked.

"Haggis," she replied.

Alfie, who was already at the table with Jayden, winked at us. "Don't ask. It involves sheep guts and oatmeal."

Jayden shoveled the meat in his mouth. "It's good—like spicy ground beef."

I tried a little on my tongue, and it was sort of nutty and salty. I couldn't decide if I liked it or not.

"Who won the cricket match?" Ellen asked.

"Weren't you there?" Alfie said, his face suddenly wary.

"It went on so long that we decided to take a hike," I said.

"Alfie won it with a smashing hit," Jayden said. "Too bad you missed it."

"There will be another time," Alfie said, winking at me.

What did that mean? I felt a blush burning my cheeks, and I pretended I needed to study the haggis on my plate.

After dinner Alfie put on his glasses again and looked at me expectantly. "I wondered if your team would like to see some will-o'-the-wisps tonight."

"What are they?" Jayden asked.

"In folklore, they're sprites that lure unsuspecting travelers into dangerous bogs, but scientists say they're really just marsh gasses. They're cool to watch."

"I'm game," Ellen said.

Alfie grinned. "Bring your torches."

"Torches?" I said.

"I forgot—you call them flashlights."

The walk down the hill to the bog was much easier with our flashlights. Alfie lingered near me. "Would you like a hand with the steep parts?" he asked.

I linked arms with Lindsey. "You lead the way, and we'll follow."

He looked disappointed but turned and started down the slope.

Lindsey was more quiet than usual, but she soon began sending her thoughts to my mind during the hike.

Peter's story makes me sad.

Is that why you've been so quiet? I formed the message so she could pick it up.

Yes. We got to talk a little more during dinner. I thought he lived free in the woods, but he's actually in prison. He can only talk with me when his guards leave because they block mind transmissions.

How does he get out?

He pulled out some metal bars, but the guards don't know.

Must be strong.

He is now, but when he woke up in prison he was too weak to even lift his hand. Couldn't remember who he was either. He's grown stronger every day. Taller, too. He started sneaking out while the guards ate dinner.

Something about this new information bothered me, and I realized what it was. *If he's being guarded, then he's not the grave robber.*

"I've been telling you that all along," Lindsey said aloud.

"Telling what all along?" asked Alfie, who was just in front of us.

I had to think fast. "Oh, we were just wondering if Oliver might be the mole."

Alfie stopped and peered at us. "Why do you say that?"

"He's always hanging around, and..." I paused, remembering we hadn't told Alfie about Oliver's life force research.

Alfie's eyes behind his John Lennon glasses blinked slowly. "He could be the mole. I'll tell MI-7 to keep an extra watch on him."

"Are they here?" I asked.

Alfie looked uncomfortable. "I'm not sure. They don't exactly let me in on their plans."

"Look!" It was Ellen uphill from us. "Did you see the light down there?"

"Everyone sit down where you are," Alfie commanded. "And turn off your torches."

The bog lay below us in the darkness, and I caught my breath at the glimmering lights that floated above the surface. Their light cast a glow on the scattered pools of water and flushed the bog mosses with an eerie radiance. "They're lovely," I said.

Too late I realized I had sat down next to Alfie. His shoulder brushed mine. "Some people believe the will-o'-the-wisps lead you to hidden treasure."

One of the will-o'-the-wisps curled up like a flame and hovered above the rest.

"A fairy lamp," Lindsey said softly.

"I could see why travelers would follow one," Ellen said. "I think if I used my dousing powers I could walk safely over the bog."

"Don't try it," Alfie said. "Downey didn't even want me to bring you this close to see the lights."

"I'm glad you did, though," I said. "They're mesmerizing, like flickering lanterns bobbing over the marsh."

"I like how you appreciate things," Alfie murmured. "I wish you would trust me."

I kept my eyes on the lights. "I do trust you."

"Enough to tell me your gift?" His hand brushed my palm, and I pulled away.

"I told you I can teleport."

"That's not everything," he said. He stood up and flicked his flashlight on. "Time to get back to Gad's Hill Place, or Downey will worry." He strode uphill, not waiting to see if the rest of us were following.

Ellen waited for me at the end of the group. "I think I know what Alfie's gift is," she said, squeezing my arm. "He's an incurable romantic—just look at the date he set up for you."

"It wasn't for me," I said loudly.

"Time will tell," she replied.

I went directly to my room when we got back—too tired for the hot chocolate Downey offered us. Lindsey went with me, saying she wanted to make sketches of the fairy lights in her notebook while they were fresh in her mind.

"How are you doing with Alfie?" she asked, her eyes on her drawing.

"I don't know. Every time he does something nice I feel like I want to run away."

"So you don't like him back?"

"Do you really think he likes me?"

"I don't know. There's something odd about the way his thoughts go crazy when he's around you."

"Any advice from your Jane Austen research?"

Lindsey glanced up from the page with her faraway look. "Trust your heart."

If it was that easy, then I knew what to do. I plumped my pillow and stretched my feet down to rest on the bedwarmer. The covers were heavy and soft, and I felt myself falling asleep when the sound of running footsteps made me sit up again. Kashmira, her deerstalker cap askew and her eyes staring, burst into the room.

Ellen followed close behind her. "You've got to hear this!" she said, her face more pale than I'd ever seen it.

"I got the hair from the giant," Kashmira said, still breathless from running. "And I just finished the DNA tests. He's not the one stealing bodies. He *is* the body!"

"I don't understand," I said.

"Think about what we've read about Professor Jaeger," Ellen countered.

"The research about healing at the cellular level," I said slowly, and my mind flew to the stitches on Peter's shaved head, the leathery skin, and the strange dragging step.

"I analyzed the hair from his hat, and it's a perfect match to the body stolen from the cemetery—DNA doesn't lie," Kashmira said.

My heart thudded painfully. "It's not possible," I said.

Kashmira pulled out a test tube and thrust it toward me. "It's not only possible—it's the truth! They kidnapped Professor Jaeger and used his research to bring Peter back to life."

"And Moulton must be one of his guards," said Ellen. "That's why he keeps showing up with his dogs."

"It's terrible." I sat down on the bed, trying to process it all.

"Poor Peter," murmured Lindsey.

"We need to figure out a way to free him," I said.

"I have a plan for tomorrow—we'll catch Moulton red-handed and save Peter at the same time," Kashmira said. "But first I've got some Baker Street Irregulars to notify." She dashed off again before she could explain further.

I didn't think I'd be able to sleep after the newest revelation, but I must have been more tired than I thought. I fell asleep instantly and was awakened around midnight by a strange moaning. I sat in the darkness listening for a while. It was like the wheezing of a dying person, and I realized I couldn't ignore it. Someone might need my help.

I followed the sound to the kitchen and found Moulton bent over old Henry, who was whimpering and breathing with an awful rasping sound. Now that I knew the truth about Moulton, my first impulse was to run back to the dorm. But if I did, he might suspect us. I had to keep up the game of being a regular camper for one more night. Alfie would be proud.

I took a step into the room, and Moulton turned an anguished face to me. If I thought he was old before, he looked ten times older now. "He's dying," he said.

Henry's brown eyes were clouded, but at the sound of his master's voice he moaned softly.

"I'm here, old man," he said, softly stroking the grizzled snout.

I sat beside him and patted Henry's rough fur. I could feel the effort it cost him to breathe. "Isn't there something we can do?"

"I've tried everything." A bitter ring in his voice made me look up.

"Stella, it's not safe for you to be here anymore," he said quietly. "Tomorrow morning I'm taking your team to the airport."

It was happening at last! Moulton was the mole, and he was making his move. Whether Kashmira wanted it or not, it was time to tell Alfie. My gut swirled, but I managed to speak calmly. "I'll tell the others to pack."

Henry gave a last long sigh and his body seemed to collapse inward. Moulton bowed his head over him, and I left him there.

I hurried back to the dorm and reached out for possibilities on the way. The vision of the snarling dogs popped into my head, but it felt inevitable now. I knew how soldiers must feel who walk to their doom, like in *The Charge of the Light Brigade*. "Theirs not to reason why, Theirs but to do and die. Into the Valley of Death…"

"Stella! I've got Peter again!" Lindsey in her fluffy night robe was running toward me, her blonde hair flowing behind her like thistle seeds. "I told Peter we want to rescue him. He's not feeling well, but he will meet us at the creek where you saw his footprints."

"First , we have to tell Alfie everything—there's been a new development."

We got Ellen and changed into jeans and sweat shirts and then pounded on the boys' door. Alfie opened it right away. He seemed pleased to see me. He was fully dressed and carrying a flashlight. "You caught me just in time," he said. "Downey needs my help again."

"Get Jayden," I said. "We've found the mole and we need to tell MI-7."

"Kashmira's going to kill us for leaving her out of this," Ellen muttered to me as Alfie roused Jayden.

"She will be glad we solved the case in the end," I said.

The boys joined us in the hallway, and I quickly told Alfie everything about our discovery of Peter and Moulton's plan for tomorrow. He didn't seem surprised. He just nodded his head and kept muttering, "good work," and "excellent deduction," and ended with "I'll tell MI-7 right away."

We snuck down to Downey's office to use the telephone since it was the only line allowed at camp. Alfie dialed the MI-7 number, but his eyebrows drew together. He took out his flashlight and ducked under the table that held the phone. "Someone's cut the phone line," he muttered. "I'll have to bike into town and find a telephone tomorrow."

"It will be too late," I said. "We have to save Peter tonight."

Alfie started to protest, but I cut him off. "If Moulton takes us away tomorrow morning, it's all over. Lindsey's our only link to Peter. We'll free him tonight and hide him in the secret room in the library until MI-7 arrives."

If Alfie was surprised to hear about the secret room, he took the revelation quite well. "Pip, pip, then," he said and led us to a back door, far from Downey. "We have the best chance of leaving the house undetected from here," he whispered. "If Downey hears us, I'll just say I was taking you with me for the errand."

"You had an errand in the middle of the night?" Ellen asked.

"It was nothing. This is much more important."

We stole out of the dorm and past Moulton's cottage without waking anyone, but half-way to the ruined chapel a dog howled behind us.

"It's Moulton," Alfie said, cursing under his breath. "We'll have to run for it."

We sprinted up the path, but the dogs must have been on our trail. The barking and snarling grew louder and closer.

≈≈

CHAPTER FIFTEEN

≈≈

"Follow me," shouted Alfie. I dashed down the hill after him to a shallow stream. "Run in the creek so they can't find your scent."

I splashed behind him, the cold water soaking my tennis shoes and my heart beating crazily.

"Jayden, can you levitate us to a tree?" he asked.

The next thing I knew, I was floating through the air to some branches that hung over the water.

"Climb," Alfie commanded, and I reached for the branch above me. I was impressed with his evasion tactics. "Now lights out," he whispered hoarsely.

The wind blew cold, and I hugged the trunk with chilled fingers. The vicious growling brought up the image of the dogs leaping at the gate, their teeth white in the moonlight.

Suddenly the snarling stopped, and I heard the dogs snuffling around the area where we entered the stream. Then Moulton's voice, "Go get 'em, girls!"

The dogs whimpered, and in the beam of his flashlight I saw them running in circles. "Come on!" he commanded and led them up the stream, playing the powerful light over the banks and trees.

I shrank back into the branches, the blood pounding in my head so loud I couldn't hear the dogs.

Moulton's voice came through, loud and sharp. "That'll do! Up the trail you go." His flashlight moved up the hill away from the stream, and I let out my breath in relief.

"Don't move till we're sure he's gone," Alfie whispered.

My feet in the wet sneakers turned numb with cold before Alfie let us climb down. Back on the ground, I swung my arms trying to warm up. The night was growing colder and the wind whipped through my thin sweatshirt. I realized too late I should have brought my jacket.

"Tell Peter we're going to approach him from the other side of the stream," Alfie said.

Lindsey clicked on her flashlight, her forehead puckered in a frown. "He's not answering."

"Turn off the light," he growled. "We can't risk Moulton seeing it."

She turned off the light, but her flurried thought came to me. *I'm worried about Peter.*

Alfie made us hold hands, and he led the way along a narrow trail that bordered the creek. If someone on the other side turned on a flashlight, we'd be exposed, and I held my breath every time I stepped on a brittle twig. The only factor in our favor was the wind, which was rising. It sent the dead leaves scraping over the ground and produced a queer whistling in the tree tops.

At last we stopped, and Alfie clicked on his flashlight. He stood in front of a huge rock. "The meeting place is on the other side," he whispered. "I need to check before we go further—how do you know you can trust Peter? Have you considered he might be luring you out here?"

"Peter wouldn't do that," Lindsey said. "He told me…"

"But what if he just told you those things so you would trust him? Is he communicating now?"

"No, but there must be a reason."

Alfie shook his head. "Too risky."

"You're wrong!" Lindsey shouted. She turned away from him and dashed around the rock. I didn't hesitate for a second. If it was between Lindsey and Alfie, I knew who I trusted. I raced after her bobbing flashlight.

We're too close to give up now. Lindsey's panic stung like a swarm of wasps buzzing in my brain. *We have to free Peter.*

The others must have felt the same way because I heard them running after us.

The meeting spot was dead ahead across the creek, and I splashed through the water, not bothering to look for stepping stones. Thick bushes stood in a clump, and Lindsey dove into them, calling Peter's name, but no one answered. She ran back to me, her eyes wide. "I can't reach his mind. Something's wrong."

Alfie caught up with us, sputtering warnings, and suddenly a huge spotlight snapped on, pinning us under its beam. "Put down your weapons," a deep voice said. "You will not be hurt if you cooperate."

"We don't have any weapons," Alfie called, his voice shaky. He lay his flashlight on the ground, and we followed his example. Two men in gray uniforms scooped them up, then proceeded to tie our hands in front of us. One of them had a gun, and he pointed it at me. "Line up and follow," he ordered.

Alfie looked terrified, but Ellen kept her nose in the air. The bright light tracked us as we walked back across the stream. I realized we were going the same direction as Peter's footprints that I had spotted during our nature hike. The cold in my hands seemed to spread to the rest of my body.

Ahead loomed a ramshackle building with a low flat roof and gray paint peeling from the walls. The guards pushed us inside and the gun guy kept his weapon trained on us.

Inside, a dim bulb illuminated rows of tables draped with sheets. Peter stood beside them, but he wouldn't look at us. His scarred head drooped on his chest, and he seemed shriveled and shrunken. Where his head had been shaved, the hair was growing back through the black stitches, giving him the look of a molting bird. He shifted away from us, dragging the one leg which now seemed completely paralyzed.

At first I thought Alfie's suspicions must be true, and Peter had betrayed us. But then I noticed his hands were tied like ours. His body shook, and he cringed in pain at every shout or loud sound.

"He's sick," Lindsey whispered to me.

"Walk," ordered the guard. He pushed Peter in front of us and opened a door. We stumbled down some stairs, and down a hallway to a cell with bars. "Lock them in," he growled.

Peter shuddered and rolled his eyes when the iron door clanged shut.

"He says this is his cell," Lindsey said. She helped him sit on a pile of hay that must have served as a bed.

"Why are you helping him?" Alfie said. "He's the reason we're here."

"No! He's a prisoner like us," she said.

"You can't trust anything he says," he retorted.

Lindsey turned her back on him. "Who is keeping you here?" she said to Peter. She listened for a moment, then narrated to us. "He said Spectacles keeps him here. She made him stronger with a medicine she gave him in a needle."

"Spectacles?" I asked.

At that moment a woman in a lab coat walked up to our cell. Fluffy white hair and spectacles—it was Downey.

❧❧

CHAPTER SIXTEEN

❧❧

I peered at Downey through the bars, hardly able to believe the transformation. Where she used to seem soft and dithering, now she was hard and determined. Her glasses twinkled in the dim light, but her smile was grim. "Welcome to the Frankenstein Project," she said.

"Frankenstein—like the monster?" I said.

She stiffened. "That is a common misunderstanding. Frankenstein was the name of the inventor."

"So you've invented another monster?"

"Monster, no. Reanimated life, yes."

Prickles went up and down my arms like ants on a roller coaster ride. "What did you do with Professor Jaeger?" I had a terrible suspicion he was already dead— another test case for her awful experiment.

"We had hoped your presence here would draw him out. He could add so much to our research."

"Then you don't have him?" Somehow, seeing her irritation at my question made me feel better.

"Get the lab equipment," she barked at the guards.

"We'll see how many questions you have once I'm done with you," she said.

The guards returned with stacks of chairs.

"Tie them up, but take that one out." She pointed at Alfie.

"Where are you taking him?" I asked.

"Not your concern." She tilted back her head to peer at me through her spectacles, giving the weird impression of a harmless old grandmother pausing from her knitting to plot evil.

A guard shoved me in a chair and tied me to it, wrapping the cords so tight, I couldn't feel my fingers. A strange contraption near the right shoulder of the chair had a needle sticking from it, and I held very still to keep away from the sharp point. While the guards worked, Downey went from chair to chair, setting a dial on the needle contraption.

"It was discovered quite by accident, you know. A serum that could reanimate corpses if infused in their veins. Professor Jaeger was a weakling—afraid to use it on humans. Thought it should be destroyed, and the authorities agreed with him!" She was behind Peter now, and she placed both hands on his shoulders. "Before they could terminate the research, I stole his specimens and infused one in our friend here." She patted Peter on the head, and he slumped in his chair, a larger version of the ones that restrained us.

"Not only did we bring the corpse back to life, but he grew larger and stronger than he had ever been. The factor is being produced and multiplied in his veins as we speak." She turned the dial on the needle of Peter's chair, a gleam of triumph flickering behind her spectacles. "Soon we will be able to reanimate an army of corpses."

"So you're using him as a human test tube."

"In a sense. We'll take his blood, but his body will keep producing more—and all of it filled with the factor of life!" She jabbed the needle in his neck, and Peter groaned. When she pulled the needle away, she bent to stare at the dial again and nodded with satisfaction. "The concentration is almost high enough for our purposes. Tomorrow we will realize our dreams. That is why it is so important that none of you are still here to get in the way." The last words were said carelessly, almost as an afterthought. "If you cooperate, we'll reanimate you with the others. And then you can help us with our little project."

"We'll never help you," I said, trying to keep my voice steady.

Her lips curled on one side in a half smile. "What if we could reanimate your parents?"

My chest felt too tight to breathe. *What was she saying?* For a moment I wanted to believe it. I could almost picture my parents alive, like in the picture in the locket. I started to reach out for the possibilities, but even before I touched them, I knew it was useless. "It wouldn't be the same," I said dully. "They wouldn't remember me."

She pounced then. In one swift movement she yanked the locket from my neck so that the chain snapped. "You care more about yourself than the life of your dear parents?"

The blood rushed in my ears, and I half rose from the chair, determined to lash out at her, but the chair was too heavy, and I fell back. She laughed. "We've been blocking your possibilities, but I think it's time to let you see the beauty of my plan."

I glared at her so hard, the room seemed to turn dark, and suddenly the possibilities began flowing in my brain.

I saw Downey in the room with the tables draped in white. In the next picture, she was lifting the sheet to reveal the shriveled head of a woman, her eyes closed. I didn't want to watch, but I couldn't stop the possibilities. Image after image of dead people, and then one that made me choke with horror—Jayden, his eyes staring in death. Then they came too fast for me to register fully. A crowd of people armed with guns, bombs exploding, buildings collapsing, lines of tanks clogging a road, until finally— the images I had seen at the airport: London on fire, then covered with smoke and finally: darkness.

Someone was yelling "No, no, no!" Over and over again. I opened my eyes and realized it was me. My friends were gathered around me, staring anxiously. Downey was gone, and they had shifted their chairs to circle me.

"We have to get out of here," I said. My heart was pounding so hard I had to gasp for air.

"It's going to be all right," Lindsey said. "Just rest a moment. Jayden has a plan."

It was hard to focus at first. The light seemed too bright, and the bars of the cell wavered. I took a deep breath and concentrated on Jayden whose outline seemed blurred. But as I watched, he became solid again and the rushing in my ears faded.

Outside our cell, a guard's jacket hung on a hook. Jayden levitated items from the pockets—a book of matches, a wallet, and a couple pencils. He concentrated on the next pocket and brought out a pack of gum and a small orange. He shook his head, disgusted. "You'd think a guard would carry a knife."

He floated the matches to his chest and struck one. The first two fizzled out, but he got a small flame with the third one and held it against the rope on his arm. It caught fire, and he winced as it burned through the rope and singed his skin.

As soon at the rope slackened, he burst out of the chair and untied Lindsey, who worked on Peter's ropes while Jayden freed the rest of us.

Peter's face was pale, and sweat ran down his forehead. He staggered to the iron bars of the cell and raised the bar on the left in its socket. I knew he had loosened it in the days when he was stronger, but he barely had the strength to lift it now. The iron bar came out of its hole and created a gap large enough for us to escape.

He groaned and sank onto the pile of hay in the corner, and a single tear slipped down his leathery cheek.

"You must come now," Lindsey said, but he shook his head.

"He says his legs are sick," she narrated.

"We'll come back for you," I said.

He looked up at me, and his brown eyes reminded me of Henry, tired and sad. He dug in the hay and pulled out Lindsey's poetry book, which he touched to his lips for a moment. Then he ripped a page from the middle and held it toward me, his eyes pleading. I stepped forward, and he pressed the page into my hands, nodding approval. I slipped it in my sweatshirt pocket.

"He says we must go now," Lindsey said.

I squeezed through the bars after the others and looked back at Peter. He was curled on the hay, clutching the book to his heart.

We snuck up the stairs, and Lindsey checked ahead for thought activity. There are three people in the room," she said. "And one of them is Alfie."

"I'll create a diversion," Jayden whispered, "and the rest of you run. Take Alfie with you, and he will know how to contact MI-7."

We crouched behind the door, and Jayden darted into the room to hide behind one of the white-draped tables. Immediately, a clanging of metal tools signaled the start of his attack.

"Watch out!" cried a man's voice.

We charged from behind the door in time to see an empty table flying through the air at Downey and one of her guards. I ran straight for Alfie. "Go!" I shouted.

He startled, and then turned and dashed for the door. We followed on his heels while tables crashed behind us. We sprinted toward the creek and all the way up the hill to the ruined chapel. "In here," Alfie called. He ducked into the grassy space surrounded by crumbling walls.

I thought we were safe, but just as Jayden caught up with us, Alfie clicked on his flashlight and pulled out a gun.

"Everyone stop there," he said, deadly quiet. "I know how to use this thing."

"Don't be crazy," Ellen said, but he trained the gun on her.

"I'm working for the Frankenstein Project, and you will do as I say."

"You're the mole?" I couldn't believe it. "You told us we were bait to find the traitor, but it was *you*."

"Don't use that word." His voice was hushed, but I could feel the rage simmering below the surface. "I know your gift, Stella. You can see possibilities—that's why they blacked out your file. But you've met your match, because I'm an illusionist."

"Never heard of it," I said, trying to sound brave.

He swung the gun to point at me, his face twisted. "I make people see what they want to see. People don't really want the truth—they prefer illusions that fit their little paradigms of the world. You, for example, want to believe that justice will prevail." He laughed bitterly. "It was easy to hijack your gift and insert a little mind loop—

a fake image of snarling dogs that came up every time you reached out for a possibility."

"But I bypassed it when we were fencing."

"That's because I was searching for your gift, and it worked."

He aimed the gun at Jayden. "I created the little people for you, and Downey delivered them for me. She was the mysterious figure in the cloak." His voice grew deeper, mocking us.

"The bees were real," Ellen said.

He snorted. "But not the ghostly voice that threatened you from the woods. That was me." He looked at Ellen. "The crossed sticks that led you off the cliff were me as well."

"You could have killed me," she said.

"I was just testing your powers. I had to know how strong they were."

"Why are you doing this?" I interrupted.

"With your gift, you should be the first to realize what our research means—the way the monster's body healed itself? No one ever has to die again."

"There are worse things than death," I said. "Like living with the guilt that you killed your friends for your own gain."

"You don't have to die if you play your cards right," he replied, the irritating twinkle coming back to his eyes. He seemed to enjoy holding the gun on us, swinging it around to point at us when we tried to speak.

The sound of heavy feet provoked a wide smile from him. "That will be the guards now, come to help you join our little project."

The spotlight sprang on again, so that every detail of the ruined enclosure sprang into vivid detail—the mossy rocks, the carpet of fallen leaves and the drooping harebells crowning the top of the wall.

"Get in there," said a guard's voice, and Moulton stumbled into our circle.

His hands were tied, and he had a purple bruise on his forehead.

≈∞≈

CHAPTER SEVENTEEN

≈∞≈

"What are you doing here?" I whispered to Moulton.

Alfie still had the gun trained on us, but he had turned to talk with the guards.

"Same as you," the old man said.

"No talking." Alfie brought his full attention back to us. "And don't try any mind stuff. The guard here will cut off any thought transference."

"Your experiment is dead," Moulton growled.

"What do you know about it, old man?"

Moulton straightened to his full height, and his shoulders suddenly seemed broader. "I'm not an old man." Though his hands were tied in front, he was able to raise them to his chin and peel away a thin plastic layer from his face, almost as sheer as skin. The wrinkles and bushy eyebrows came away with it. "I'm Professor Bruce Jaeger."

Alfie took a step back, eyes wide, and gripped the gun more fiercely. "Tell Downey to come at once," he told a guard.

"You won't kill me," the professor said, taking a step toward him. "I'm the one who found the serum."

"Not a step closer," Alfie screamed. "Guards, tie them up."

More guards appeared from the shadows. They pushed us against the ancient wall and tied our hands. Another guard held back the professor.

"You're making a mistake, Alfie," the professor said.

"I know what I'm doing," he retorted. "This is the greatest breakthrough in the history of the human race, and I plan to be the first to give my body to science."

Ellen squinted at him. "You really believe this stuff—"

"Alfie, listen to me," Professor Jaeger cut in, and now his voice grew deeper, more urgent. "Henry was my first test case. He was with me all through school—a gift from my big brother—"

He paused, and I suddenly saw pictures in my mind of the puppy Henry and a young version of the professor running in a sunny field. The pictures quickly slid forward—the professor at college with a full-grown Henry, throwing a Frisbee to him in a park, sharing bits of a hamburger with him at an outdoor café. I didn't need his explanation to know what happened next, but he continued, speaking earnestly to Alfie. "I couldn't bear to part with him when he died. I knew the serum ought to be destroyed, but I broke down and used it on him. At first he was like a puppy again—running after balls, chewing on my shoes. He grew larger and stronger than he had ever been." The professor smiled, but his eyes were sad. "Then something went terribly wrong. In a single week, the serum aged him. I watched him die all over again.

You must know the serum is not life but death." He choked on the last words, and for a moment Alfie lost his confident grin.

But then he shook his head and leveled the gun at the professor. "You're only saying this to keep me from my destiny."

"I'm telling you the truth."

"They will reanimate me if I die again," Alfie said.

Downey ran into the grassy enclosure, followed by the guard. "You found him? Where?" She caught sight of the former Moulton, and her face turned red. "You! I knew someone was spying on me, trying to wreck my work."

"There will be no army of reanimated corpses to fight for you," Professor Jaeger said calmly.

"You're wrong!" Downey stomped toward him. "I've already brought the first hundred to my laboratory, and the serum is complete."

As she spoke I thought I heard a dragging step in the shadows near the entrance, but I couldn't see anything, and with disappointment I realized it must have been the wind, which whistled over the top of the ruined walls and sent dead leaves whirling and scraping around my feet.

"We are ready," Downey announced, her voice shrill. "Bring the corpse collection system."

Alfie put his gun in the holster and walked toward me. The guards formed a line in front of us. Two of them kept their guns trained on our group, but the other six took out long leather cases.

"They will deaden us one at a time," Alfie said, a crazy gleam in his eye. "It won't hurt. They are using Samoan poison darts—a quick paralysis and then death. And no permanent damage so that when we are reanimated we will have healthy bodies."

He reached out and touched my hand, and I shivered. "I will go first," he continued. "Think of Dickens's words—it's a far, far better thing I do than I have ever done."

"Alfie, no—" I knew he wasn't thinking clearly. I'd seen Henry die, and I knew the professor was telling the truth.

He gripped my hand then. "Don't worry, dear heart. We will be together forever."

The guards held long wooden blowpipes to their mouths—every one pointed at Alfie with the deadly darts loaded.

"Now!" Downey's cry came harsh in the moaning wind.

I caught a quick movement from the shadows, and Peter launched himself in front of Alfie with an amazing burst of super-human strength. He turned as he fell with six darts struck in his chest and a look of sublime joy on his face.

The poison acted quickly. His body shook in one great shudder, and he lay still.

"What have you done?" Downey shrieked. She caught up one of the heavy blow pipes and ran at the guards, striking at them. "Get the antidote!"

We ran to Peter, and Lindsey cradled his head. "Hang on, Peter," she yelled. But he was gone, his scarred face at peace and a faint smile on his lips. She bent low over him, her tears falling on his leathery cheek.

A ferocious barking heralded the arrival of dozens of men and women in black suits. Kashmira was in the lead. "Good dogs," she shouted. They bounded back and forth between the professor and her, jumping up to lick him on the face and then frisking back to her for a pat of approval. "Down, girls," she shouted, and they sat at the professor's feet while she untied his hands. The black suits swarmed around the guards, removing weapons and slapping on handcuffs.

Downey fought them, even after the handcuffs. "I will have my army," she shouted over and over. It took three men to lead her away.

Alfie was taken with the rest, his head hanging low. He stole a glance back at Peter as he left, his face a mixture of shame and grief.

A far, far better thing I do… The words came back to me now, but with a different meaning than Alfie intended.

꿍꿍

CHAPTER EIGHTEEN

꿍꿍

The black suits began the process right away of returning the bodies in the laboratory to their cemeteries, which apparently spanned the whole length and breadth of England. But Peter came from the graveyard in Chesterton, and we buried him there the next day.

The bell tolled solemnly in the crumbling belfry of the church as we gathered. The crooked headstones of the cemetery gave me the feeling of standing off-balance, but one stone stood straight at the head of a neatly-dug hole. Someone had tried to scrape away the moss and lichen, but the only word that could still be read was: Peter. Who had he been? When did he live? There was much more to him than that slab of stone.

The weather had grown bitingly cold in the night, and I dug my hands into the warmth of my coat pocket, clutching the page Peter gave me in the cell. I understood now why he wanted me to have it—so that I could read it at his funeral.

Lindsey laid the book of poems on the coffin, and Kashmira added the goldfinch nest. The fragile interlacing of twigs, still lined with soft thistles, reminded me of

Peter and his love for poetry and other delicate things. Their beauty touched his soul.

The priest came out from the church and read a psalm, and we sang a hymn. Last of all I read the poem. It was by Robert Louis Stevenson:

> Under the wide and starry sky
>   Dig the grave and let me lie:
> Glad did I live and gladly die,
>   And I laid me down with a will.
>
> This be the verse you 'grave for me:
>   *Here he lies where he long'd to be;*
> *Home is the sailor, home from the sea,*
>   *And the hunter home from the hill.*

We left the church, and the bell rang again, clear and sad in the chilly air.

We returned to Camp Dickens, which hardly seemed the same place where we had arrived a week ago. Gray clouds scudded across the sky, and brown leaves had caught in the hedge that lined the road. Most of the trees were bare now.

The Doyle boys, wrapped in winter coats, ran after our car as we pulled up to Gads Hill Place. The smallest boy waved a mittened hand that glimmered with something gold.

"Irene! It's your locket. We found it near the stream!" He triumphantly presented me with his prize and the others shouted *Huzzah!*

"The dear old Baker Street Irregulars," Kashmira said, and I thought I detected a tear in the corner of her eye. "They were still spying on you last night, and thanks to their information I called in MI-7."

As we settled around the peat fire in the parlor for cold sandwiches and biscuits, I was still puzzling over all that happened.

"Kashmira, how did you make contact with MI-7 if the phone line was cut?"

"You should be a detective," she countered. "See how your intuitive powers have grown? The simple answer is that I had my own phone." She patted her ever-present sleuthing suitcase. "MI-7 posted me here when Alfie started acting erratically. Didn't show up for an important briefing, couldn't account for a few hours here and there. Downey is his aunt, by the way."

"That explains a lot," I said.

"She was passed over for a job at MI-7 and never got over it. The International Human Project recruited her, and she went to the University of Edinburgh to study cellular biology along the lines of Dr. Jekyll's experiments with changing human nature. She never discovered the formula to transform people, but she got a grant from the Mary Shelley Foundation and met

Professor Jaeger through it. We know now that she learned about his breakthrough in restoring life, and she stole his research and all the serum. We thought Professor Jaeger was kidnapped as well, but you know the real story."

Moulton joined us at this point, or rather—the professor, looking young and fit. His two dogs scampered at his heels.

I bent down to pet them, and they wriggled around to lick my face.

"I'm taking them for a walk. Care to join me?" he asked.

I walked with him along the cobbled road, the dogs racing back and forth from one interesting scent to another.

"I'm going to miss them," he said.

"Don't they belong to you?"

"No, I borrowed them from the real Moulton—an old friend of mine who was kind enough to let me impersonate him. He's having a spiffing time in retirement, sailing the coast of Cornwall."

"So you have the gift of impersonation?"

"You might say that. It has other applications as well, but that's classified by MI-7." He winked.

"Does it allow you to sneak in and out of places undetected?"

He raised his hands in mock defeat. "I guess there's no keeping secrets from someone who can see possibilities."

The dogs trotted into the chestnut woods and we followed them. Behind us, the Baker Street Irregulars were trying to sneak along the hedge, snapping twigs and whispering exclamations when they momentarily lost sight of us.

I picked up one of the brown nuts that carpeted the ground. "You're the one who left the conkers for us," I said.

"Did you suspect it was me?"

"No—I only guessed there was a connection with Buckeye since we call these buckeyes in our country."

"I opened the book to give you a clue about my research and left the newspaper article as well."

"Were you the one removing all the articles on the life force?"

"No. I was trying to track the thief, and that's why you saw me rummaging through desks in the Austen dorm."

That made sense. "Did you plant one of your essays there as bait?"

"How did you know?"

"We thought we were tracking *you*."

He chuckled. "All of us off on the wrong trail. Oliver was helping me, by the way, but we never caught the thief."

From the chestnut woods the dogs wandered down the slope behind Chawton Cottage and brought us to the bog. They sniffed around the edges, flushing out a water vole and scaring away a flock of black birds. The yellow moss covered the hidden pools, deceptively still as solid ground.

"You never suspected Downey?"

"Funny thing. I totally underestimated her powers."

How like this bog our adventures in England had been. Hidden traps and dishonest friends. The yellow moss was withered now from the night's frost. As we left I turned back for a last look and caught the glimmer of a hidden pool.

The Baker Street Irregulars gave up their spying on the walk back and ran with the dogs, throwing them sticks and crying *huzzah* when they retrieved them. We joined the others who had piled the suitcases at the front door in preparation for our departure.

Oliver was explaining an intricate point about cricket to Jayden, and Lindsey was listening in, though I knew she didn't care a bit about sports. Near the car, Kashmira was trying to convince Ellen to go into detective work. "With your dowsing powers you would be terrific."

Ellen blushed. "It sounds fun, but after visiting England I'm thinking about going into archaeology. I never understood about the layers of history before."

The professor announced it was time to go, and reluctantly we got in the car. Oliver was driving us as far as the station, and the professor would accompany us to the airport. Kashmira and the Baker Street Irregulars clustered round for a last farewell.

"Good-bye, Irene!" they shouted as our car pulled away.

"Come back and help us solve another mystery!" Kashmira called.

I waved at them and looked back at Gad's Hill Place with its weathervane twirling in the autumn wind, and I hoped I could return soon.

I still had lots I wanted to do in Great Britain—museums, houses, and famous places I wanted to see. I had lots of questions too, but one was more urgent than the others. Professor Jaeger was sitting in the seat facing us. I brought out the article he had left me in the window seat. "I was wondering—why did you dedicate your research to us?"

His eyes twinkled mischievously. "I wanted to thank you for saving my life all those years ago. Buckeye told me the whole story. I didn't suspect I'd need your help again."

"I'm not sure we helped that much."

"Sure you did—you made contact with Peter and drew out the bad guys."

Ellen punched me in the arm. "We were bait, after all!"

Professor Jaeger frowned and a touch of worry flickered across his face. "After Henry died I feared for your safety, and that's why I planned to leave with you next morning. After I buried Henry, I went to check on you and you were gone. The dogs helped me track your trail, but I wasn't able to catch you in time."

"I thought you were planning to abduct us—proof that you were part of the gang imprisoning Peter."

"I didn't know you made contact with him. Even with the dogs, I hadn't been able to find him. I'm sorry to put you in danger."

"We didn't mind the danger," I said. "I think the hardest part was Alfie's betrayal."

"What will happen to him?" Jayden asked.

"MI-7 will work with him. They may be able to reform him yet."

At the station Oliver said good-bye, and I thought Lindsey might swoon when she shook his hand, but she bore up admirably. She had sewn a net bag and filled it with petals from the flower he gave her at the vintage ball. I noticed her sighing over it as she tucked her things away in the train compartment.

The doors slid shut, and the train glided out of the station, gathering momentum until the familiar blur of teleportation grew around us. We zipped through the mouth of the tunnel and the lights went black. Another moment of roaring speed and before I was expecting it, the half-circle of light popped into view. We were back at the secret station at Westminster Abbey.

We climbed the stairs to Poet's Corner, the same group that started this journey, minus Alfie. I hoped that wherever he was, he was becoming a new person. Peter's sacrifice had changed me. I knew it had the power to change Alfie if he let it.

Ellen was carrying a late-blooming rose from the garden, and she laid it on the grave of Charles Dickens. Kashmira had given her a copy of *A Tale of Two Cities* as a parting gift. It was tucked under her arm for another reading on the plane.

In front of the Jane Austen inscription Lindsey did one of her fancy curtsies, and Jayden and I threw out a few Shakespeare insults at the bard's statue.

"Deboshed fish," I murmured.

"Mouldy rogue," he countered.

I turned to Professor Jaeger. "Where are Robert Louis Stevenson and Sir Arthur Conan Doyle?"

"They're not here, but there are always activists working to get their favorite authors memorialized in Poet's Corner."

The quiet hush of the stone columns and soaring roof seemed to soak into my bones with peace. "There's a lot to remember from this trip," I said.

"Let memory be ever golden," he said softly.

"Dickens?"

"Pure Jaeger, I'm afraid."

❧

The voyage home was a lot less exciting than the trip to England. Niner met us at the London airport. He had been debriefed on all that happened, and he hovered over us like a mother hen. I didn't have the heart to tell him he was too late.

The plane circled around London as we took off, and this time I saw only a peaceful city with the criss-cross of streets and avenues dotted with cars, buses and people going about their business.

In my mind flashed a picture of Peter, who died to keep all this possible. The people down there didn't give him a thought. How could they? But for me, there would always be a place in my heart for a poetical giant who knew "it was a far, far better thing" to give himself for others.

I opened my locket and looked again at the picture of my parents smiling at me from the miniature photograph. I understood now why they did what they did. I let the locket rest in my palm, and I remembered.

ABOUT THE AUTHOR

Joyce McPherson is the author of books for young people as well as a director for Shakespearean theatre. She is also the mother of nine children, who give useful advice for her stories. She has never been to Camp Hawthorne, but still hopes for an invitation someday.

ACKNOWLEDGMENTS

Thank you to the moon and back to all the teachers, librarians, and bookstore wonders who have placed a copy of this book into the hands of a young person. And to all the bloggers who have spread the word, and to all the fans who have shared your enthusiasm with me and others, THANK YOU! I would thank you all by name if I could!

A special thank you to Garth, Heather, Alexie, Duncan, Andrew, David M., Grace, Connor, Luke, Emily, Laurie, Sally, Cathy, Marilyn, Laura, Kashmira, David Y., Meg, Tanya W., Jonathan, Elena, Kat, Lauren, Alexis, Catherine, Rachael, Lindsey, Mira, Jenn, Mary, Maria Luisa, Jenifer, Taylor, Kathleen, Jason, Wren, Von, Verne, Alejandro, Billy, Priscilla, Jessica, Louise, Tanya C., Andy, Michelle, Towana, Kim, Charles, Jane, Mette, Amanda, Ann, Andrea, Margaret, Debbie, Beth, Carolyn, Rich, Andrew, Alexandra, Eileen, Jess, Lisa, Gail, Mat, Connie, Lois and many others who read, listened and cheered this book to completion.

Made in the USA
San Bernardino, CA
26 December 2017